SHADOWS ALONG THE ICE

Judy Baer

Forever ❀ Romances

is an imprint of
Guideposts Associates, Inc.
Carmel, NY 10512

This Guideposts edition is published by special arrangement with Judy Baer.

SHADOWS ALONG THE ICE
Copyright © 1985 by The Zondervan Corporation

ISBN 0-310-46962-7

Edited by Anne Severance
Designed by Kim Koning

Printed in the United States of America

CHAPTER 1

"YAHOO!"

Pam Warren winced and shot a daggered glance at the cigar-chomping reporter next to her in the *Winnipeg Star* press box. He was so ebullient that she had difficulty concentrating on this final period of the Blazers' game. Though not well-versed in the rules of hockey, even she could see that player number 48 had saved the game with his hard-fought final point.

Raising his stick high in the air, the skater, clad in red, white, and blue, gave a victory sign as his teammates ushered him from the ice in one body. Pam tore her eyes from the hero of the moment and spoke to the whooping, whirling man next to her in the press box.

"He's very good, isn't he?" she ventured.

"Good? Good! Lady, he's the best center the Blazers or any other professional hockey team has ever *had!* Where have you been all winter to just be noticing that now?"

"In Arizona, actually. Where I grew up. Pamela Warren is my name. I'm the new sportswriter for the

Winnipeg Star." Pamela extended a slim, finely manicured hand to the paunchy, red-faced fellow.

Grabbing the slender fingers in his beefy ones, he sucked deeply on the unlit cigar and said, "So you've never seen old Tiger skate before? Well, you've had a treat tonight! He's never been better!"

"This 'Tiger'—is that the same as Mr. Tyler Evans, the man I have listed on my interview instructions? I was told to interview a Tyler Evans after the game. He's expecting a reporter from the *Star.*" Pam studied the chicken-track scrawls of her editor, wondering anew what she was doing at a hockey game on her first night in the city. Her bags were still packed in the trunk of her car while she found herself here, edging with a stocky stranger toward the Blazers' dressing room.

"Tyler—Ty—Tiger. Whatever. Tie 'em to their seats Evans—he's one and the same! You'll never find another hockey player like him. What a man! Your editor must have a lot of confidence in you. Mine would never waste an interview with Ty Evans on a dame!" With that, her burly partner veered toward the dressing room.

Fighting the crowd to follow him, Pam bit off an answer. This assignment had been purely accidental. She would already be in her new apartment by now if the sports reporter assigned to Tyler Evans hadn't called in sick just as Pam had stepped into her editor's office. She had begun to regret reporting her arrival to her new employer. And regret turned to self-reproach as she heard the threads of conversation floating from the locker room.

"Here comes the press! Better put your clothes back on!"

"Nah! Give 'em something to talk about!"

Crude language and laughter, which made Pamela's eyes widen in dismay, emanated from the dressing room as she shadowed the hefty man she had met in the press box. Mortified, she realized that there was only one other female reporter muscling her way into the room. But that hard-faced lady seemed oblivious to the bawdy jokes coming from the half-naked men on the benches.

Pam shuttered her eyes in alarm as a bare-chested man in only a towel shot toward the shower room. She could only imagine her parents' horror if they suspected the situation in which she found herself. It was a rude contrast to the sheltered, unsullied existence she had always known.

Prickles began creeping along her hairline as Pamela felt eyes watching her. Glancing around the congested locker room, her gaze fell on the one quiet player in the room. He was utterly composed in the midst of chaos. Aware of her riveting stare, his compelling, golden eyes locked with hers, and much to her chagrin, he began shedding his clothes—slowly, purposefully, daring her with his eyes to turn away.

One glove followed the other to the floor, tumbling across the already discarded helmet. He pulled the shirt over his head, somehow maintaining the magnetic gaze that held Pamela fast. Methodically he undid the laces of his protective padding, and the bulky gear dropped to the ground, and Pamela found her eyes resting on a broad, blond-furred chest.

Mortified that she had not looked away, Pamela shook herself from the hypnotizing stupor the man had engendered and cast her eyes discreetly to the floor.

Hoping he had forgotten her presence, Pam looked up only to be met once again by catlike golden eyes. She struggled against them, swimming in the golden, green-flecked orbs, drowning.

Suddenly those eyes opened wide in surprise as a bottle of champagne was dumped unceremoniously over the tousled blond head. Pam breathed a sigh of relief as the player turned his back to her and pursued the offender, playfully protesting. Grateful for the reprieve, she sought her only acquaintance in the room.

"Well, you got your questions ready?" Her cigar-chewing colleague was at her ear.

"Not really. I'm rather unprepared. I thought we'd talk about the game," Pam stammered, thankful for a diversion.

"Listen, lady, Ty Evans doesn't grant interviews often. Don't waste your time with that. Go for a scoop. Something about his personal life. From what I hear, he could give you an earful."

"I don't even know which one he is," Pamela complained, glancing over the celebrants, thankful her father didn't know where she was. She was sure he wouldn't approve.

"You don't know Ty Evans? Then why have you been staring at each other ever since you walked into the room? Don't give me that, Lady. Ty Evans saves *those* looks for women he knows well—really well, if you get my drift."

Stunned, Pamela shrank against the wall. No doubt about it—she had already made a fool of herself in the eyes of the man she had come to interview. Now her mind couldn't formulate a sensible question if her life depended on it. Panicking, she turned heel, poised for flight. She couldn't turn in a story on this man. She couldn't even face him.

"Going somewhere?"

The golden gaze had her trapped again. Droplets of water rained across his shoulders from his showered head, beads collecting in the furry hairs of his chest. Barefoot, he wore only trim-fitting slacks and a narrow leather belt. Pamela found herself staring anew.

"I need to leave. I shouldn't be here." she stammered.

"Why? You have a press tag. The press are always in here after an important game." He shifted from one bare foot to the other, and the thick muscles of his chest rippled in the artificial light.

"I'm only here by accident. It's not my original assignment. Maybe we could talk on the phone. I'm sorry, but I have to leave now." Pam shook her head and backed toward the door.

"Hey! Are you from the *Star?* I've been wondering who was going to do the interview! Wait till I get dressed, and we'll get out of here. Maybe we could get a cup of coffee while we talk. Do you mind?"

Mind? Pamela's brain screamed. She could have hugged him in gratitude. She wanted nothing more than to be away from this raucous, unfamiliar atmosphere.

Outside in the hallway, Pamela leaned against the concrete block wall and willed her trembling legs to be still. Tonight she had already seen and heard more of what her father labeled "the world" than she'd experienced in twenty-two years as a pastor's daughter. The small Christian college she had attended had its share of team sports, but she was convinced that the language in their locker rooms was vastly different from this one.

As she stood with eyes closed, her first sign that she was not alone was the fresh smell of lime and soap whirling in her nostrils.

"Ready?"

Pam's eyes flew open. Before her stood Tyler Evans, golden boy of the Winnipeg Blazers, wearing a bulky Irish sweater. His hands were jammed deeply into the pockets of his slacks, pushing back the front panels of a resplendent calf-length raccoon coat.

Words stuck in her throat and she found herself gaping at the masculine sight before her. "A . . . but . . . yah . . ."

He smiled briefly, apparently accustomed to his

11

effect on women, and replied, "Okay, then. Let's go."

Taking her by the arm, he steered her from the arena by a back passageway used only by the players and arena employees.

The bitter chill of the air slapped her back to her senses, and Pam found herself shivering as they stepped into the night.

"Cold tonight, I hear," Ty commented tersely. "Radio said it would get to minus twenty-nine degrees before the night is over."

"Is that Fahrenheit or Celsius?" Pam chattered, not really caring, knowing only that it was far colder than she had ever before experienced.

"Celsius. It's minus thirty-five or so degrees in Fahrenheit. Are you from the States or something?"

"Uh-hum." Pam shivered. "Arizona to be exact. I didn't know anywhere but the Arctic Circle had weather like this!"

Ty laughed. "This isn't so bad. It's a fairly still night. When the wind blows, *then* it feels cold! Why do you think everyone up here wears fur coats?"

"Well, I've never liked the idea of killing animals for profit and vanity, but—" and an icy blast hit them as they came around the corner of the building, "— maybe it's not such a bad idea after all!" Her sturdy cloth coat seemed made of paper, and the boots that had seemed ridiculously warm in Arizona felt like plastic slippers on her feet.

"You want to drive your own car or come with me?" Ty had his hand on the door of a little red Porsche and was looking at her inquiringly.

Against her better judgment, knowing she should never get in a car with a total stranger, Pam stammered, "I'll go with you. My car is several blocks farther down. I'd freeze before I could get there."

Ty nodded and ushered her into the soft leather interior. That, too, smelled of lime. Pamela noticed him working with the front of the vehicle for a moment before he slipped into the driver's seat and flipped the ignition. The car sputtered to life. Momentarily Pam could feel gusts of cold air spurting from the heating system.

"It will warm up in a minute. Where do you want to go?"

Baffled, Pam replied. "Why, I don't know. I've only been in Winnipeg three hours, and most of that time has been at the *Star* and the arena. Where do you want to be interviewed?"

"*Three hours?* You've only been here three hours and you're already working? How did that happen?" Ty took the initiative and pulled from the parking lot.

"I stopped at the newspaper office on my way into town to introduce myself to the editor and tell him I'd arrived. I drove from Arizona and didn't want them to be concerned about me. Just as I got into his office, the sportswriter who was to interview you called in sick. So he gave me the job." Pam huddled over the front heater, which was finally breathing gusts of warm air. "I arrived at the beginning of the third quarter. I had to park about a mile away. It was a very exciting game, though—what I saw of it."

She could feel rather than see Ty shaking his head. "And where do you plan to stay tonight? On your new desk with a typewriter for a pillow?"

"The paper rented me an apartment. They said it was close to the downtown area, only a couple blocks from Portage Avenue, wherever that is. Are you familiar with it?"

Ty hooted at the question. "Portage Avenue is hard to miss. The early residents of this region carried their boats from one end of what is now Winnipeg to the other, from the Red River to the Assiniboine, hence, Portage Avenue. Now it's one of the main thoroughfares in Winnipeg. You really *are* new, aren't you?"

Pamela was feeling more displaced by the moment.

13

"Do you mind if I eat while we're talking?" Ty inquired, glancing sideways at his companion for the first time.

"No. Not at all," she assured him, surprised that he would ask.

"I rarely eat before a game. I don't want it to all come up if I get jammed in the stomach. Like crepes?"

The man was certainly straightforward, she decided. Maybe an interview wouldn't be so difficult after all. "Sure, but it's your decision. I stopped and had a sandwich about four o'clock."

"Well, it's nearly eleven. I think you could manage to join me. We'll go to a place that has an after-theater menu. They all serve dinners until one or two AM." He pulled into a parking lot across from a massive gray building with one dimly lit door.

Pam's eyes darted to the right and to the left. The street seemed empty and threatening. Suddenly her parents' warnings began coming back to her, and when Ty ushered her through the door, she breathed a sigh of relief. They were inside a cozy cave of a room with sloping walls and dark, discreet tables nestled underneath.

"Good evening, Mr. Evans. Good game. May I take your coats?" The hostess greeted them. Pam's eyebrows raised in the dim light. She was obviously in the company of a Canadian celebrity.

"Hi. Can you give us a quiet table near the back?" Ty requested. For a moment Pam found herself flattered, and then she remembered that she was here to work. Sharing a cozy table with Tiger Evans would be a one-time experience.

While following him down the long corridor of tables, Pam studied his light, athletic walk. He was power and muscle from head to toe. Ty pulled out a chair for her, leaving Pam to face the dining room, and he took the chair that left his back to the crowd.

Instinctively Pam realized that he didn't care to be recognized. Adoring fans could ruin a meal—or an interview—rather quickly.

Service was instantaneous when one was dining with a celebrity, Pam discovered. An effusive waiter hovered nearby, and Ty had only to lift a finger for the man to be at his side, eager to serve.

"What do you want to eat, Miss . . ."

"Warren, Pamela Warren. I have to apologize, Mr. Evans. I don't know what you think of me, coming here with you like this. I suppose it's very unprofessional, but my head is still swimming with the newness of it all. You're being very kind."

Ty chuckled. "I do so few interviews that this could be standard procedure for all I know. I surprised myself by agreeing to this one. Got caught at a weak moment, I suppose."

He shuffled restlessly in the chair, obviously uncomfortable talking about himself. Pam studied him discreetly through the dark fringe of her lashes. She noticed a faint scar running from cheekbone to jaw across his right cheek. It gave him a rough, rakish air that was both attractive and repugnant. The men she had known had obviously not lived life in the manner of Ty Evans. The bawdy locker room still clamored in her memory and the daring manner in which he had removed his clothes, more amused than concerned that she was watching.

"What would you like?" Ty broke into her thoughts.

Pam blushed as she glanced up, hoping those golden eyes couldn't read her mind. "Hot tea would be nice. I'm chilled to the bone."

"No food? I hate to eat alone." He smiled openly for the first time, showing an even expanse of white teeth and a deep rugged slash that could barely be called a dimple in each cheek.

Pamela melted. "Whatever you recommend would

be fine with me." Perhaps food would undo the heady feeling she was experiencing.

"Earl Grey for the lady and coffee for me. With extra cream," Ty began. "And two bowls of French onion soup, two orders of crepe ratatouille, and crepes suzette for dessert."

Pam's eyes widened. Ty's idea of a simple meal was vastly different from hers. She fumbled in her purse for a notebook and pen, but before she had it opened, Ty began an interrogation of his own.

"So, then. How does it happen that you came from Arizona to Winnipeg—and in December, of all months?"

Pam smiled. "I have a degree in journalism and a special interest in sports writing. Once I graduated, I decided I wanted to see the world. I've lived a rather cloistered existence. It was time to get away. A friend heard of this position, and I applied. More amazing yet, I got it. And here I am." She spread her hands wide, a bemused expression crossing her heart-shaped face.

"And is hockey your specialty?" Ty stirred his coffee, tapped the spoon on the rim and laid it down on the table, intently watching her all the while.

Laughing nervously, Pam shook her head. "No. The closest I've come to a hockey game is in the books I've read. Arizona isn't the best place to find a hockey team. But—," she hastened to assure him, "—I'm a very good writer and a fastidious researcher. I'll do your story justice!"

Amusement flickered across his features as he leaned back in the chair. "I'm sure you will, Miss Warren. I'm sure you will. Now what do you want to know about me?" Somehow he had managed to make the casual question seem personal and intimate. Pam found herself blushing like a school girl.

The cigar-chewing reporter of the early evening came unexpectedly to her mind. His advice rang loudly in her ears: *Go for a scoop. Something about his personal life . . . he has lots of stories to tell.*

For the first time since they had been seated, Pam glanced around the room. Quickly she discovered that most eyes were on their table, and the fevered buzzing of conversation no doubt included her and Ty Evans. The women especially seemed interested in the broad back and dark gold head exposed to their vantage point. A knot grew in Pamela's stomach. How could she ask a man like Ty Evans about his personal life? And if he were willing to tell her, would she really want to know?

"Well, aren't you going to ask me anything?"

"Uh, well, since I'm so new, maybe you'd better tell me a little about your background," she stammered.

His golden eyes darkened to the color of maple syrup. "What I want the public to know of my background is already public record, Miss Warren. Why don't you ask me something original?"

Pam bit her inner lip until she tasted her own salty fluids. Perhaps she deserved the cut. Where was the courage that had made her the *Arizona Tribune's* most feisty investigative reporter?

"You'll have to forgive me, Mr. Evans, but your fame didn't reach as far south as Arizona. You'll have to give me some information, whether you like it or not."

"Touché!" Ty grinned. "I deserved that. I must admit reporters make me rather nervous. They're sort of like doctors, prying at your innards with pens instead of scalpels, but cutting you up, nevertheless."

Immediately more sympathetic, Pamela began her work, trying to slice from Ty's mind the information that would constitute a "scoop" for her new employer.

A frustrating quarter hour later, Pamela knew no more about Tyler Evans than she had at the beginning of their conversation. He thwarted her every stinging question, answering blandly, revealing nothing.

Finally Pamela became irritated. Forgetting all her father's admonishments toward civility and gentilesse, Pamela blurted, "From what you've told me tonight, Mr. Evans, I can deduce that you are as exciting as a piece of milk toast and as opinionated as a sponge. Come on, *Tiger*, you have a rough and tumble, masculine image to uphold! There's got to be more to you than this!"

"Rough and tumble, huh? Masculine, they say? So that's my image. Well, well. And I've disappointed you? So sorry. Do you want me to see what I can do about that—Miss Priss?"

A startled tremor slithered through her as Pam realized that Ty had put his words into action and slid his hand across the table to grasp her own.

She immediately regretted her abrasive words and pulled her hand onto her lap. She was sorry for her abruptness when Ty raised an eyebrow and studied her thoughtfully. He was to be under scrutiny, not she.

Just then the soup arrived, and Pam breathed a sigh of relief. Ty Evans kept her off guard, just as he did opponents on the ice. She was glad for the respite.

Bowing her head to give thanks for the food, she could feel golden eyes boring into the top of her sun-blond hair. She raised her eyes to meet his and found them filled with gentle amusement. Inexplicably she felt the need to defend her prayerful actions.

"Excuse me, but I always say grace before meals. I—"

"You don't have to make any excuses to me, Miss Warren. I don't make any for my actions. You shouldn't have to either. I believe your habits are purer than mine." Ty shifted in the chair, stretching his long legs until they grazed Pam's.

"But I thought—"

18

"Act on what you believe. Don't apologize for it. I never do. I respect people who stand up for what they believe. Don't move to Winnipeg and change that about yourself, Miss Priss. I think that's what I'm going to like best about you." Ty smiled that genuine, unguarded smile again and nearly took Pam's breath away.

She reached shakily for her notebook and jotted the words "animal magnetism" onto the page. Whatever she wrote about Tiger Evans, that phrase would have to be included. There was no other way to explain the charm he exuded. Whatever the "scoop" turned out to be, it would no doubt stem from that magnetism.

Aloud, Pam responded, "Thank you for that. I'm glad to know you believe as I do—"

"Oh, I didn't say *that!* Don't get me wrong. Just don't compromise yourself here in the big city. That's all." Ty chuckled, obviously amused that she had thought him to be a believer.

A finger of disappointment marched down her spine. She was already wishing desperately for a Christian friend in this unfamiliar place. Then the cold light of reason came back to her. How dare she think of Ty Evans as a friend! How presumptuous! How unreasonable! He had consented to do an interview with another reporter and gotten her instead. She had begun to mistake politeness for friendliness. And for a moment he had made her forget how alone she was in the city that was to be her new home. Sadly she turned to her meal. Perhaps food and some sleep would settle her rocketing emotions.

They finished the meal in silence; Ty, lost in thoughts of his own; Pam, wondering how she'd make a story of the infinitesimal scraps of information Ty had given her. She wouldn't make a very good showing her first time out.

"Well, ready to go?" Ty's voice broke into her weary thoughts. The day had been a long one.

"Yes, please. The meal was wonderful, but I'm getting very drowsy. I left Sioux Falls, South Dakota, at seven AM, and now it's after midnight."

"No wonder you look like you're about to cave in. Come on. I'll drive you back to your car."

Pam stopped at the till on her way past, but the waitress said, "Oh, madam, Mr. Evans took care of your meal. Everything is paid for."

She caught up with him in the front entry, shrugging into the lustrous fur coat that made him look like a giant bear, "Mr. Evans, I meant to pay for our meal. This was my interview, remember?"

Ty chuckled. "If I don't like the article, I'll bill you. Come on, now, bundle up. They say the temperature has been dropping steadily since we got here."

Pam shuddered as they stepped from the warm cafe. The wind had increased, and an icy blast whirled around her legs and under her cotton skirt. Ty seemed oblivious to the tempest and sauntered toward the Porsche. He held the door for her, and she scurried inside away from the arctic howlings.

"Have you quit shivering yet?" Ty asked as they neared the arena parking lot. Her car was the only one left in the lot, now empty and quiet.

"I'm afraid I'll never get used to this," Pam's teeth chattered so much that the words were nearly unintelligible.

"Sure you will. And this year you'll see a white Christmas. It's worth a little cold."

"I don't know," Pam muttered, her face buried in the front of her coat. Her body was trembling with a violent force. "I'm so cold I'm not sure I can get my key in the ignition."

"Well, I'll wait here until you get the car started. Can you find your way to the apartment?"

"I have the address, and now I know where Portage Avenue is. I should be able to find it. Thank you, Mr. Evans. It was very nice to meet you." Pam shimmied

20

from the car and ran toward her own. Once inside, she fit the key into the ignition and turned it to the right, waiting for the comforting growl of the engine springing to life.

Silence. Nothing. Tears came to her eyes, and the two that fell to her cheeks hung there in frosty dismay.

"Troubles?" Ty was at the window, his big fur coat buttoned high under his chin against the wind.

"It won't start."

"We should have moved it to my parking space and plugged it in."

"Plugged it in to what?"

"Plugged in the headbolt heater. So it would start. You *do* have a headbolt heater, don't you?"

"I'm not sure. What does it look like?"

Ty glanced at the car's front grid. "No headbolt heater. Well, I'll give your car a jump. Stay where you are."

Pam shivered in the cold vehicle as Ty pulled his car up to face hers. Pulling cables out of the trunk, he lifted the hood of her car, obscuring the view.

"Now try it," she heard him yell. Shortly her own car sprung to life and he slammed the hood into place. As he returned to her window, she could see frost on his eyebrows and the tips of his hair.

"Thank you. How did you do that?"

He grinned like a frosty polar bear. "Tomorrow you get this jalopy to a garage and have them install a headbolt heater. And from now on, whenever you park the car for more than a few hours, plug it in. There will be outlets in all the parking places at your office and apartment building. This isn't Arizona. And another thing," he continued before Pam could get a word in, "get some warmer clothes. Buy a snowmobile suit or sleeping bag to put in the trunk of your car. If you ever had trouble in that flimsy stuff you're wearing you'd be a Popsicle before anyone found you.

21

Now give me that address, and I'll show you where you live. I wouldn't sleep tonight if I left you in the parking lot to find your own way home."

Not waiting for Pam's gratitude, he trudged to his own car and pulled into the street. She followed, thankful that she didn't have to make one more decision on her own. If she'd found herself lost tonight, she would have wept in dismay. Independence was beginning to seem more charming in theory than in actual practice.

Shortly the Porsche pulled in front of a tall building with large wooden doors. Ty jumped out and came to her window. "You've got indoor parking here. Follow me up the ramp. Since your apartment is on the tenth floor, I'll park on ten if there's a space." He disappeared into his car, and the car pulled away again, turning into the serpentine ramp.

By the time they were parked, Pamela's legs were shaking so she could hardly stand. Nervousness and exhaustion were finally taking their toll. Ty took the keys from her shaking fingers and opened the trunk, pulling the top cases from its interior.

"Is there anything else in this car that you can't get along without tonight?" He looked like a furry beast of burden under all the cases he'd managed to balance.

"No. That's most everything. It's supposed to be a furnished apartment."

"Okay. Let's go then."

Her key unlocked the security door, and they stepped into the hot, dry air of the hallway.

"Your apartment must be this way." Ty led her to the door and she edged the key into the lock. The door swung open and she stepped inside.

"Welcome home, Miss Warren." His voice was very close to her ear, and it was all Pam cold do to keep from jumping. The tiny apartment stood before her, simple but inviting. It was better than she had expected after the harrowing day she had had.

"Not bad. Small, but it will do the trick. Hope you didn't bring a lot of clothes." Ty was peering into the single closet.

Pam laughed weakly. "I don't own many, and most of those are totally inappropriate for the weather. I'm afraid I don't have anything suitable to wear to shop for new ones!"

"You're only a couple blocks from stores interconnected by indoor ramps. Make it that far and you'll be all right. Just go out the north door and turn left. Cross the street and there you are. Are you going to be okay tonight?" Ty Evans turned and studied the shaking girl before him.

"Yes. Thanks to you. How can I show you my appreciation for all you've done?"

"Be kind in the article." Ty winked and strolled toward the door. "I'd better be going. We have a game tomorrow night, and I need some sleep. Welcome to Winnipeg, Miss Warren." With that he gave a wink of one golden, catlike eye and closed the door.

Pam sunk to the floor in exhaustion, finally releasing the emotions she had been so carefully hiding. Tears of loneliness dripped forlornly down her cheeks, and she uttered a prayer to the Father she had been talking to all the way from Arizona, *Oh, Lord, what have I gotten myself into now?*

CHAPTER 2

PAM SQUINTED AT THE LIGHT FILTERING through the frost-encrusted window and groaned. Burrowing her nose into the pillow she attempted to block out all thoughts of cold and snow and winter.

"Nobody told me it would be *this* cold!" she muttered. Perhaps no one in her home town knew that *anywhere* could be so glacial. At least not anywhere inhabited by human beings. She had shivered through most of the night, unable to warm after her forays into the wind.

Slipping out of bed, her feet landed on the toasty floor. "At least my thermostat works!" she said aloud. The needle was buried at the right side of the disk, sending the temperature in the room somewhere into the eighties. Ignoring the bare walls and jumble of suitcases at the front door, Pam pulled her warmest clothing from the hang-up bag Ty had placed in the closet. Hunger was gnawing at her insides, and she needed to be up and going. She had only today to get settled. Tomorrow was Sunday and Monday she had to have the interview on her editor's desk.

"What interview?" she groaned, hitting her forehead with the heel of her hand. Tyler Evans had evaded all but the most mundane questions, drawing her out instead. He should be the one writing an interview—about the *Winnipeg Star*'s newest employee.

She had just pulled on her only pair of wool blend slacks and layered a turtle-neck, a blouse, and cotton cardigan over it when her door bell rang. Puzzled, she peeked through the peephole before answering. Before her was a slim young woman with straight brown hair and large blue eyes.

Pamela opened the door without releasing the chain and peered around its corner. "Yes? May I help you?"

"Are you Pamela Warren?"

"I am. And who are you?"

"My name is Wendy Williamson. My father is Richard Williamson. He was a seminary student with your father."

A wave of relief flooded through Pam. Her father had located his old friend after all.

"Come in, Wendy. I'm sorry for the bolted door, but, being a stranger and all . . ."

The slim girl smiled. "Your father sent a message when he called. He told us to tell you to keep your doors locked. I guess he didn't have to worry."

"My father is more than a little overprotective. Letting me leave Arizona and come here was the hardest thing he's ever done. He wasn't going to do it until he remembered that your father had a church here. Then he decided perhaps there would be someone to look in on me."

"I checked here yesterday since that's when your father said you might arrive. You must have come in very late."

"After midnight. And not without problems. I pulled my sheets out of a suitcase, made the bed and

25

fell into it. Now I was trying to find my warmest clothing so I could brave the weather and go find breakfast."

"I'll take you out for breakfast and grocery shopping, Pam. But what did you say about problems?" The slender girl's face creased in concern.

"Apparently my car isn't equipped for Canadian winters either. Ty—I mean, a man told me that I needed a headbolt heater, whatever that is."

Wendy laughed, "And antifreeze and de-icer and a storm kit if you go back on the road. Welcome to the land of *real* winter, Pam. I doubt your car will even start this morning to get it to a garage. My brother owns a gas station over on Ellis. After breakfast I'll call him, and he'll take care of it for you—headbolt heater and all. Where's the car parked?"

"Level ten, slot ten," Pam recited, overwhelmingly grateful for her father's friends. Between them and Ty Evans, perhaps she would get settled without mishap after all.

"Do you need anything for the apartment besides food?" Wendy inquired, studying the hastily dumped pile of luggage at her feet.

"A shower curtain and a few more towels. And a new wardrobe. I discovered last night that mine is grossly inadequate." She could still feel the wind cutting through her jacket like it was paper.

"If you'd like company, I have the entire day free to take you around. My father promised yours that we'd help you get settled. And I love to shop. I don't come uptown as often as I'd like. It would be a treat for me too."

Pam could have hugged the girl. The desperate loneliness had abated somewhat with her arrival. "Wendy, I'd like nothing more. Can you get me to food and clothing without going outside?"

"No, but it's only two blocks to both. Come on." They ran pellmell into the biting wind and finally

26

into the first level of an uptown shopping mall. Pam's face felt as if she had been slapped, and catching a glimpse of herself in a mirror, she found she looked that way too. Her cheeks were bright and rosy, and the tip of her nose a flaming pink.

"How can you people stand it up here?" she murmured.

"We're used to it. You'll soon like it too. Here's a muffin shop. Is that enough for your breakfast or are you the steak-and-eggs type?"

"Muffins are perfect."

Two date-nut muffins and four mugs of steaming coffee later, Pam and Wendy were browsing in the shops.

"Well, as a native, what do you recommend I buy?" Pam inquired of Wendy.

Picking up a thick knit sweater, Wendy held it in front of her new friend. "This is one hundred percent wool. That's a wise choice if you're cold."

"But won't it itch?"

"Wear a blouse under it. Layering keeps you much warmer. Actually a good pair of boots and a down coat should be your first choices. Come on. I know where you can find beautiful ones."

It was three-thirty in the afternoon when the pair, laden with packages, returned to Pam's apartment. Not until after Wendy had promised to pick her up for church and departed did Pam notice the slim white envelope on the floor near the front door.

Curiously, she tugged at the flap. Inside was a single ticket to tonight's Winnipeg Blazers game. A scrap of paper floated from the envelope as she shook it. In bold black pen scrawl were the words: "You need to see a game from the beginning. Tiger."

Pam smiled. Maybe he was right. She still didn't have a good angle on her interview. Watching him on the ice might be her answer. And this time she was ready for the weather.

Meticulously she laid her purchases across the bed. She planned to wear a good share of them to the game tonight. First she arranged several pair of heavy woolen knee socks, then three wool sweaters in teal, violet, and creamy ivory. Next Pam arranged the woolen trousers and coordinating blouses in a row. Her new down coat with matching hat, scarf, and mittens blended with the rainbow array on the bed and only the thick, flat sherpa lined boots seemed as dreary as the weather outside. Finally, with a sense of embarrassment, she pulled out the two items she had purchased while Wendy called her brother about the car.

First out of the package came a set of ladies' thermal long johns. Even the dainty butterflies and pink and yellow flowers couldn't hide their purpose. But after last evening, Pam was determined never to be so cold again. Last, but far from the least of her purchases, was a large poster. She pulled it from its tube and spread it across her bed.

Into her eyes from the polished page stared Tiger Evans. Decked out in his cumbersome hockey finery, helmet and chin strap in place, leaning fiercely onto the blade of his stick, ready for the puck, to sail his way across the ice, he was a handsome and intimidating opponent. The scar she had noticed last night had been retouched on the photo, accentuating it to increase his awesome visage. Even the massive equipment couldn't conceal his handsomeness.

Scooping up the long johns and the poster, Pam carried them to the closet. They were the two purchases she would make sure no one ever knew she had made.

After hanging the new curtain, she showered and took special care with her hair. It fell with casual abandon to her shoulders. Studied nonchalance was the look of the moment in Arizona. Because of the winter hats she hadn't been able to judge what was current here.

28

Wearing several layers of her new clothing, including the wonderfully warm long underwear, she sat down at the kitchen table to write. The least she could do was get her jumbled thoughts down on paper. Perhaps that and tonight's game would help her with the article.

At six o'clock, after a slice of toast and a cup of tea, Pam went to the main floor of her building and called a taxi. Tonight she wouldn't risk being stranded in the cold. Tiger Evans wouldn't be there to bail her out.

She strolled with the crowd into the arena and found her way to an usher who pointed her to a seat on the blue line at the center of the ice. Apparently when Tiger Evans asked for a ticket, he got a good one. She settled into the seat and watched the crowd.

People swarmed up the yellow ribbons of stairs, most to the red seats circling the ice and some to the cheaper blue seats above, so high Pam wondered if the air up there wouldn't be too rarified for her. Glancing through the Yearbook she had purchased, she discovered that there was seating for fifteen thousand. All but about ten of those seats seemed to be filled tonight.

She gazed down at the ice. The Blazer logo was imprinted in the ice in red and blue, and the clear, primary colors stood out like a beacon against the frozen whiteness.

Flipping through the booklet, Pam came upon Ty's picture in the line-up and some chatty information for his fans:

Tyler (Tiger) Evans—Number 48
   Centre/Left Wing
   Shoots Left 6'2''—200 lbs.
   Born: Winnipeg, Manitoba
   February 25, 1958
   Last Amateur Club:
   University of North Dakota

Her eyes skimmed the lines searching for more of what she didn't know about Ty Evans. Bits and pieces jumped out at her from the page. "A fan favorite and the Blazers' leading scorer . . . tenacious player and strong leader . . . appointed team captain for third consecutive year . . . a graduate of University of North Dakota School of Business, Evans holds an MBA . . . son of a Manitoba furrier . . . enjoys swimming and weight lifting . . . Tiger is single."

Pam's eyebrow shot upward. She had learned more from the brief blurb than from nearly two hours in his presence. Now she knew as much as the rest of his fans might. What new angle could she present on a figure as public as Tyler Evans?

"Let's hear it for the Blazers!" boomed across the arena.

The string of players skated one by one onto the ice as their names flashed across the midair score board. When Tiger Evans's name glimmered into view and he skated nonchalantly into line, the crowd roared. Pam felt herself being caught up in the excitement.

Just then the announcer came across the sound system and the crowd rose in unison for "Oh, Canada." A faint twinge of loneliness shot through Pamela. She had even left the "Star-Spangled Banner" behind in her quest for independence.

Conjuring up every scrap she had ever read about hockey, Pamela recognized the face-off. With a clack of sticks the puck was in play.

Three players rolled into the boards battling over the vulcanized disk, and Ty slipped it away for a pass shot to a waiting man. The crowd roared as the puck sailed into the net. The next two periods held her spellbound and made her regret that she had never had the opportunity to skate.

Entranced by the skaters' grace, Pam was shocked when violence erupted in the third period sending four players into the penalty box. Sticks and fists flew until the referee broke them apart. And at the midst of the fray was Tiger Evans.

The game ended with an impressive powerplay, and fans were still shaking their heads as they poured into the aisles.

"Another good game, eh? That Evans, he can really skate!"

"Yeh, and fight. Scrappy character, ain't he?"

"Sure looks that way on the ice. You never read much about him though. Keeps to himself, I hear."

Pam guiltily skulked behind the two. Ty had piqued her curiosity. He had become more than an assignment.

"Will Pamela Warren report to the Press Box. Will Pamela Warren report to the Press Box." Startled, Pamela veered to the right and jogged toward her destination. Could something be amiss? She couldn't remember mentioning to Wendy that she would be here tonight. Had something happened to one of her parents?

"I'm Pamela Warren, and I just heard myself paged . . ." she puffed into the attendant's face. "Is something wrong?"

"Not that I know of. This message just came up from the locker room."

He handed her a sheet of crumpled paper: "Pamela Warren—Wait for me in the Press Box—Tiger."

She sank into a chair in relief. For a moment she had imagined the worst, her family seeking her out all over the city to report a tragedy. It took a moment before she realized the import of what was happening. Ty Evans wanted to see her again!

"So you came."

Pam jumped at the sound of his voice. The press box had emptied, and a lone janitor was sweeping popcorn and paper cups from the floor. Her wonderfully warm clothes had made her sleepy, and she had nearly dozed off in a chair.

31

He seemed bigger and even more handsome tonight. He wore a powder-blue cable-knit sweater and a pale blue turtleneck over tight, faded jeans. His rusty corduroy suitcoat flapped at his hips as he stood studying her, hands jammed deep in his pockets. His hair was damp and curling at his neck.

"I'm sorry I'm late, but I had trouble getting to the showers. There was a little celebration in the locker room tonight."

"It was a wonderful game."

"We won. I guess that's what counts."

"You don't sound very happy about it."

Ty chuckled. "Any time I end up in the penalty box, it makes me cranky."

"Looked to me like you might have deserved it." Pam retorted, remembering the brawl that Ty had spawned on the ice.

"That has nothing to do with it. Hockey players have a bad reputation for being fighters. I'm gentle as a lamb." He pulled his hands from his pockets and spread them innocently before him. Somehow, Pam didn't believe a word of it.

"And what did you want to see me for?" she inquired, her curiosity getting the best of her.

"I wanted to make sure you hadn't frozen to death, for one thing. Looks like you went out and bought some sensible clothes." He stared at her sweater clad body until she began to squirm uncomfortably. Those golden eyes had X-ray qualities.

"Thank you for your concern. But now that you've seen for yourself that I'm alive and thawed, I'd better be going. They seem to be closing up the place."

"I didn't drag you out here just to look at your new clothes."

The tone in Ty's voice made Pam stop and spin around.

"How about dinner?" He continued, satisfied that he had her attention. "No games for a couple days. Tonight I can stay out late."

And what was last night? Pam wondered to herself. Whenever she was up past midnight at home it seemed late to her. Her father thought it decadent to laze in bed past seven AM. This morning had been a real luxury.

All the warnings about city men and innocent young girls her parents had given rang out in the back of her mind. But she wasn't as young as her parents seemed to think she was. And Ty was far more of a gentleman than he had needed to be. Even her father couldn't have faulted him last night.

"Thank you for asking. I'm surprised that you wanted anything to do with me after the fiasco of last evening."

Ty's chin quivered in amusement, but he didn't laugh. "Did you take care of your car?"

"Yes. Headbolt heater, antifreeze, de-icer. All but a sleeping bag. I'm not planning on leaving the city until the weather improves. It *does* improve, doesn't it?"

"Considerably. At least sixty degrees—a hundred, Farenheit," he translated. "You'll have use for those Arizona clothes yet." Ty shifted his weight from one foot to the other. He seemed more graceful on skates than on terra firma.

"Good! If it hadn't been for the ticket you sent, I never would have left the apartment. The thermometer read eighty-two when I left and it was marvelous!"

"I'll pick a warm spot to eat. In fact, I know just the place." The golden glow flickered as he blinked. "Come on. I'll take you to your car. Just to make sure it starts."

"I didn't drive this evening. I took a cab. I didn't think I'd be lucky enough to have you come to my rescue twice."

"Then you'll come with me. Better yet." Ty gave her a look that sent shivers down her spine. A predatory, hungry look. A look Pam was unaccustomed to in the men she had dated. Suddenly she didn't feel quite so safe. Ty Evans was more of a man than she had before encountered. She didn't know what he would expect of her as a woman.

Instinctively, she pulled back, but he caught her arm. Trapped. The odd moment passed as Ty smiled. "Come on. I'm starved."

Tonight Pam knew what Ty did at the front of his vehicle before he got in. He unplugged the heater from a wall outlet. The car sprung easily to life.

"Have you had a chance to look around today? Or was all your time spent shopping?"

"Actually, a family friend showed me how to do my shopping without going outside. I managed to spend all my money under one roof. My time in the taxi was spent praying we wouldn't slide into the car next to us."

"Then we'll take a spin down Portage and up some side streets just to give you a feel for the city. And I'll try to drive carefully on the ice."

They pulled into traffic and Pam leaned forward, attempting to look every direction at once. As they neared downtown she exclaimed, "Look at all the banks! Every block has one or two! And fur stores! I've never seen so many in my life!"

"You can understand now that you've had a taste of the weather, can't you?" Ty asked, amused.

"It did seem rather barbaric and vain at home, but somehow it's becoming more sensible by the moment to wear a fur. By the way," and she paused hesitantly, "I noticed in the write-up that your father is a furrier."

Ty nodded briefly but did not expand. A shuttered look hooded the golden eyes. Pam felt an icy wall, more chilly than the windfall between them. Then he shook himself and the grim look fell away. Obviously his father was another topic Ty Evans wouldn't discuss.

34

Anxious to change the subject, Pamela peered out the car window for a topic. "Oh! There's the Bay. Is that the place I've heard about? Is that the Hudson Bay store?"

He nodded and inquired, "Do you know the history of that store, Pamela? Do they teach that in Arizona?"

"Wasn't it a trading post of some sort where the first trappers sold their furs?"

"Yup. It had a charter from the King of England to build a company here in the wilds of Canada. It's come a long way since that first outpost."

"There's so much to see and learn!" Pamela exclaimed. "I hardly know where to begin."

"Glad to hear you're interested. That means you might stay a while," Ty commented blandly, giving Pam no hint at any hidden meaning behind the words. She felt like a Yo-Yo on a string, alternately drawn to him and spun away.

"Here it is."

They were in front of another unprepossessing looking building. Ty seemed to like restaurants tucked into unexpected niches. As they got out of the car he amazed Pamela by swinging the big fur coat off his back and around her shoulders.

"Here, try this for a minute. See if that convinces you that furs are practical." He didn't even shiver in the bitter night air.

Pam felt enshrouded in a wall of warmth. Everywhere the coat surrounded her, no wind could touch her. It was nearly as cozy as her overheated apartment but for the wind whipping about her ears and feet. The warmth from Ty's body made her snug and the heady smell of soap and a limey cologne assaulted her nostrils. It was wonderful.

"But aren't you cold?" she asked the man beside her.

Seeming unaware of the temperature, he edged her

toward a door. "Well, I won't give it to you for the night, but I thought you'd like to know how it felt." Pulling the door open, he steered her toward a flight of spiral steps leading to a basement. At the end of the stairs was another door.

In her curiosity, Pamela had almost forgotten that she had Ty's coat draped across her shoulders until she saw the patrons of the small bistro staring at her. Ty was easy to recognize and more than one starry-eyed fan was attempting to decipher who was wearing his coat. The maître d' rescued her, whipping both Ty's coat and her own into the back.

Tiny booths dotted the perimeters of the room, each heavily shrouded with thick draperies pulled back to reveal the candlelit tables.

"Something private—and warm," Ty told the maître d' and they were led to a secluded booth away from the door.

Pam's eyes widened when she saw the prices on the menu. One paid dearly for warmth and seclusion in this place.

"I, ah, I'm not very hungry, really. I had toast and tea before I left the apartment. Maybe just coffee."

Amused understanding crossed his features. "I'll order for you, Miss Warren. I'm not afraid of the prices." Again Pam was struck with the forthrightness of the man. He never equivocated and always called things as they were. He had an air of honesty about him and rather than lie he chose not to speak at all. Her father liked an honest man.

Pulled back to the moment by a waiter's voice, Pam listened as Ty ordered.

"Sea food cocktail, please, and a soup. The beef broth with egg custard is fine. Tossed salad with oil and vinegar dressing. Broiled veal T-bone steaks, chives butter, and steamed potatoes. You can bring the dessert cart by when we're done. And," Ty smiled wolfishly, "you can pull the drapes after we're served."

Nodding, the waiter backed away leaving Pam to stare at the man across from her.

"You just spent my whole week's wages ordering dinner!"

"Fortunately for you, *I* did the ordering and *I'll* pick up the tab. If you want to treat, don't take me out after a game. My appetites are voracious then—all of them."

Pam shrank against the leather bench. Perhaps she had made a mistake after all. Ty was moving much more quickly than she liked. She didn't want to be guilty of leading him on. Her sheltered upbringing hadn't prepared her for a man like him.

"Ty, my agreeing to have dinner with you, well, it doesn't mean—"

"Sorry if I scared you, Miss Priss. Tigers are like that sometimes. I'll stay in line. I promise." But his leg edged closer to hers under the table.

Relieved to see the food arrive and the topic change, Pam eagerly spread her napkin across her lap. When the last tray arrived, the waiter discreetly pulled the heavy brocaded curtains, leaving them completely alone in the little alcove.

"When you say warm and private, you *mean* warm and private, don't you?" Pam commented, uncomfortably aware of the intimacy of the situation.

"Tiger's always have a lair, don't they? I imagine people think of my apartment that way sometimes. Just pretend you're trapped. Give up and enjoy. The wind's still cold and blustery outside. Be glad you're here."

She *was* grateful for where she was, safe and warm. Prayerfully, she bowed her head to give thanks for what had been given her. When she raised her head Ty was staring, his dark blond head cocked to one side.

"Why do you do that?" There was no mockery in his voice, only curiosity.

"To give thanks for what I've been given. I feel richly blessed, Ty. I need to say thank you."

"Does your whole family do that?" he inquired.

Pam nodded. "My father is a pastor, my mother, a musician. But I was ten years old before I realized that people played organs anywhere but church."

"Like hockey games?"

"Right. Like hockey games. My family is very strict. Even stifling, perhaps. Still, they've given me a rich religious background. But it was time for me to be out on my own and test my strength."

"And your faith?" He always cut to the heart of the question.

"I trust that it will grow stronger with testing, Ty. I'm sorry if this all sounds very odd to you but—"

"Don't apologize, Pam. Never apologize for your faith. Stand up for it. Even when bums like me ask stupid questions. Just because I don't agree with you doesn't mean you should apologize. I like people who stand up for what they believe in." He smiled then, dropping the subject.

Pam's heart was pounding in her chest. Ty hadn't scoffed. Perhaps he would be open to more conversation on the subject. But tonight wasn't the night, she soon realized, as he began reliving the evening's game.

"Brock Madsen made a heck of a pass tonight, didn't he? I never thought he'd pull it off, but he did it."

"Which one is this Brock?" Pamela's brain scanned the pages of the yearbook she'd studied.

"Number thirty two. Good skater."

"Do you mean the fellow who didn't wear the helmet?"

"That's him. He's great on passes."

"Why didn't he wear a helmet, Ty? Isn't it mandatory? That seems very dangerous to me."

"It's his choice. I wouldn't play without one. Don't have enough brains to get any more knocked out."

Pam gave him a disparaging look. "Be serious. You mean he doesn't have to wear one?"

"No. Even though helmets have been around for ninety years, it's only recently that a majority of the players have been wearing them. You know, only NHL players who signed their contracts before 1979 are permitted to play without wearing one. I guess Brock likes to feel the breeze through his hair. Says he's going bald and doesn't want to hurry the process. I tell him he's flirting with danger. Hockey players get busted up too often as it is. Without a helmet, it could be deadly."

A shadow passed across Ty's face and a pall settled on the conversation.

"Have you ever been hurt, Ty?" Pam inquired timidly, almost afraid to break the brooding silence.

"Jammed my wrist once, but other than that I've been lucky. I'm an old man in hockey. I'll be glad if I can get to retirement without a serious injury."

"An old man! You're only twenty-eight!"

"You did read the yearbook, didn't you?" Ty laughed wryly. "Five more years and I'll be ancient history, probably. Then I'll be stomping the streets for work."

Pam could see the sadness in his eyes. Even Ty Evans had things to fear—injury, age. All those worries hung like shadows between them. Then Ty purposefully changed the subject.

"Enough of that. I think I'll be able to scrape by on my business investments. And someone, somewhere should want a banged-up hockey player with an MBA to run their business. What are you going to be doing in five years, Pamela Warren? Editing the *Winnipeg Star* or off saving unchurched natives from themselves?"

He struck close to Pamela's dream, but she bit off her response. He had been very nice all evening and she didn't want him to ruin it by making fun of her

39

now. Ty couldn't understand what he hadn't experienced and she needed time to pray about how to approach him. He was a wilder and more sophisticated male animal than she had ever before approached.

"Want dessert?"

Pam could only shake her head no. She would be full for a week as it was.

"Do you dance?"

Again she shook her head.

"I should have guessed. Sorry. What *do* you do after midnight when you're out with a fellow?"

"Usually go home. My father always waited up for me."

"Well, Daddy's not here tonight. Come on. I'll show you the night life in Winnipeg."

Once out on the street, Pam attempted to explain to Ty that she wanted to go home, but before she uttered three words, they were interrupted by a bawdy bawling from down the street.

"Tiger! Hey, Tiger! We've been looking for you, old buddy!"

"Hey, who's the chick? Not bad. Not bad at all!"

Pam watched three burly men stagger their way. When they got close to the pair they started punching Ty playfully in the shoulders. He grinned and pushed the closest away, nearly causing him to tumble. Pam could smell the alcoholic vapors from where she stood.

"Knock it off, you guys. Go party somewhere else." Ty cajoled.

"Look who's not good enough for us tonight! Finds a good-looking dame and forgets all about his buddies!" The tallest of the three threatened to become maudlin.

"Go home and sober up. I'll see you about noon. Can't you leave a guy and his date alone?"

Pam's ears perked up at the word "date." So he did consider her a date, after all!

"Hey! The Tiger has plans! Let's let him get on with them. Sorry, buddy, didn't mean to hold up the fun!" The three weaved off down the sidewalk, hooting and making snide remarks.

Pam's heart suddenly felt more cold than her exposed cheeks.

"I'm sorry about them, Pam. Just forget it. They're decent guys when they're sober," Ty apologized.

"And would you be with them if you weren't with me?" she inquired icily.

"I don't know. Does that matter?" Ty responded.

Suddenly Pam felt tears sting at the back of her eyelids. It was all too much for her to understand. How could she be so attracted to a man so wild and unlike herself? What had come over her? There was no way to compete with that lifestyle. Whatever Ty Evans was, he wasn't for her.

CHAPTER 3

"FORGET IT, PAM. They're just having a little fun. Come on." Ty pulled her closer to himself as they started toward the car.

"Since when has that type of behavior been fun?" Pam's voice held a sneer.

Ty looked at her with mild amusement. "Since booze was invented, probably. Don't look so condemning, Prudish Pamela. Don't knock what you haven't tried."

"Is that your philosophy of life, Ty?"

"More or less. Why?"

"Then why don't you come to church with me in the morning? You can't knock it until you've tried it."

Ty hooted until two passersby turned to stare. "Prudish Pamela, you are too much! If we hadn't just met, I'd think you were making attempts to tame this old Tiger. Tell you what, I'll keep my buddies away from you and you keep church away from me. We'll stay on neutral ground. Deal?"

His proposition was met with silence. Pam couldn't agree to that, she knew. Ty needed what she had to offer, whether he realized it or not.

Her silence finally prodded him to change the subject. "Hey, Pam. When do I get to read the big interview we did last night? Whatcha gonna say about me?"

His tone was flippant, but Pam could read a twinge of concern in the playful question. Ty Evans didn't want to be exposed to the public except in the areas that he chose to reveal.

"Tuesday's paper, I suppose. I'll turn it in Monday morning. Unless my editor doesn't like it."

"So what did you write about?" Ty asked curiously. He was so interested that he nearly forgot to open the car door he was holding.

"You, of course."

"But what about me?"

"A writer has to write what they know about, Ty. I couldn't make anything up. You spent the evening with me. Figure it out." Pam felt impishly perverse. Let him worry a bit. Don't let him know she was as baffled by the story as he or that it was still unwritten. Then, with a blinding flash, the proverbial light bulb came on in her brain. The scoop! She had it. She would write *exactly* what she knew about Tiger Evans!

"What are you grinning about?" he asked suspiciously.

"Just thinking about your response to my article. I wonder if you'll like it."

Ty shot her a warning glance. "I'd better, or it will be the last interview I ever give. And, by the way," he paused and cleared his throat, "tonight is off the record, isn't it? I never know with press people what's sancrosanct and what's not."

Pam eyed him sympathetically. "Tonight's off the record. I guess I forget what it must be like being a celebrity. Having everyone trying to get a piece of you for themselves."

Ty nodded. "It makes you wary. I just don't want you to disappoint me, Pam."

They rode in silence to her apartment. Much to Pam's relief, Ty seemed to have forgotten his offer to introduce her to the nightlife of Winnipeg. Their conversation about the interview and Pam's invitation to church had subdued him. Ty walked her to the door and stretching out his palm for her key, opened it. Before he could step inside, Pam nudged her way across the entry.

"Thank you very much for the ticket to the game and for the wonderful supper. You've been more than kind. Good night." She breathed the words in rapid succession, eager to get them out before her will dissolved and she asked him inside.

"Aren't you going to invite me in?" Ty asked, suddenly seeming hurt and vulnerable, posed in a pseudo-dejected stance at the door. It was obvious that he was accustomed to invitations for a nightcap.

"It's very late, and I'm planning to go to church and Bible study in the morning—"

"I won't stay long."

"I really should wash my hair and take a bath—"

"I'll make my own coffee."

"I need to write a letter to my family—"

"I'll post it on the way back to my apartment."

"I give up, you win!" Pam laughed. His persistence on the ice obviously carried over into his personal life.

He smiled the smile that deepened his dimples to depthless valleys. The scar whitened a bit against his golden skin, and he looked fearsome and vulnerable at once. Shrugging out of the big coat, he tossed it across the tufted chair and turned to face her.

"All right. Where's the coffee pot?"

"Since you managed to talk your way in here, I really should let you do it yourself, but all I have is instant. And I'd rather not have you bumbling around in my kitchen. I think you're wider than it is."

"I'm rather light on my feet, for a big guy," Ty offered as he threw himself across the davenport in her living room.

"So I've noticed," Pam called from the cubby hole of a kitchen. Momentarily she was carrying two steaming mugs to join him. He had made himself at home, filling the tiny room with his presence. He lay across the couch, his head resting on crossed arms behind his neck, his feet crossed at the ankles and projecting over the other end of the couch. His coat filled the only chair and left Pam one of the two straight-backed dinette chairs.

Seeing her eye the situation, Ty uncoiled from his resting spot and sat upright. He patted the cushion next to him and gave her an inviting look.

Warning bells clanged in her brain. Pam knew she should stay across the room, away from that beckoning glance. But it was only for a cup of coffee. She had purposely only half filled the cups to hurry Tiger on his way. She sank down on the couch, but as far as possible from those sturdy, muscular legs.

"Are you expecting more company?" he inquired.

"No. Why would you ask that?"

"You seem to be saving room on the couch for a crowd. I was just wondering." The innocent look never left his face as Pam began to laugh.

"You do make me a bit nervous, Ty Evans. I don't quite know what to make of you."

"I can tell. But I have never eaten alive a single woman from Arizona. I want you to know that. Does that make you feel any better?"

"No, considering that leaves women to be gobbled up in forty-nine other states and numerous provinces. You probably haven't had time to get to Arizona."

"No, not yet. But I'm delighted that it came to me."

Somehow, Ty had managed to tuck his coffee cup around the corner of the couch and insinuate himself closer to Pam without her realizing it. His knee was now brushing hers, and she felt the tips of his fingers grazing the silken ends of her hair.

She was wedged between the thick, high arm of the couch and Ty. And neither object had any inclination to move.

"You have beautiful hair, Pam." The fingers were weaving their way higher, skimming lightly across the nape of her neck. "Like sunlight. You don't see many brown-eyed blondes. A nice combination, I think."

Nervously, Pam picked at the hem of her sweater. The men she had dated had always come to her parents' home. Her father's presence had always reminded them to keep a distance. Now her father was over a thousand miles away, and she was with a man who wouldn't be intimidated by her father if he were in the same room. She felt very much on her own. And unsure of what to do about it.

"Ty, I really think you should go ho——" As she surged forward in a bid for escape, Ty's right arm came round in front of her, trapping her against the couch. Her darting eyes stared across his broad right shoulder until he closed them with a kiss.

Then the room began to dance and spin with the fury of an Indian rain ritual, and Pam struggled for air. Ty Evans picked up where all the other men she had known in her life left off.

"Ty!" She was surprised by the shot-gun sharpness of her own voice.

"Hmm?" He had leaned back against the couch and was studying her lazily, obviously less affected by the kiss than she.

"You've got to leave now. You really can't stay any longer. I told you—I have things to do." Pam was surprised by the quavering of her tone. Her lips and cheeks still burned from his kisses, but the fire was not unpleasant.

Ty traced a pattern up her arm and across her shoulder. When he began drawing a delicate map across the line of her collarbone, she jumped upward.

"Go home!"

"Don't pay any attention to me. I'll stretch out on the couch. Go take a bath and wash your hair. I don't mind." He yawned lazily like a jungle cat and settled bonelessly into the couch.

Pam had the foreboding sense that perhaps other women *had* bathed in his presence, but she wasn't going to be one of them.

"Get out!"

"What about the letter to your parents? Don't you want me to mail it for you?"

That was what she deserved for prevaricating. He had turned her little lies back on her. Another lesson learned about Ty Evans—never attempt to deceive him.

After that discovery, Pam pleaded with him, finally honest. "Ty, you've scared me witless. I know I'm twenty-two years old and should be able to take care of myself. But when you kiss me like that I'm afraid I can't! My father monitored my social life like it was a space launch. The good-night kisses I've had suddenly seem more like a handshake and a wave after what you just did. Please, Ty. I'm not used to this. You'd better find a woman who is."

Ty used his dimples again, but didn't try to touch her. He unfolded from the couch and stood up. His sleeve brushed her as he reached to get his coat and sent new spasms up Pam's arm.

It was not until he stood at the door ready to depart that he spoke. "Okay, Pam. I'm sorry if it scared you. I'll try to slow down. Although," and he added the last words under his breath, "I thought I *was* moving slowly. I'll have to shift into park!"

Pam leaned weakly on the closed door when Ty had left. She had more to learn than she realized. If all the men she met up here were like Ty, she would have to be on guard every second. He could steal her heart in a moment—and break it in the process.

Wendy was already waiting by the time Pam got to the front door of her apartment building.

"Hi! Have you been here long?" Pam inquired.

"About three minutes. You're right on time. I rarely come uptown on Sundays so I wasn't sure of the traffic. It's very quiet."

"Is your father's church far from here?"

"No, not really. I'm so glad you agreed to come. We're starting a new Bible study this week, too. It's the perfect time to join us."

"What are you studying?" Pam asked eagerly. Here's where she felt at ease.

"Simon Peter. It should be an exciting study. He's an interesting figure in the Bible."

"What's the focus, Wendy? Or is it just a general study of his life?"

"No, it's about Simon Peter as a man. How human he was and yet how God was able to work through him for so much good. From what Scripture says, he had quite a personality!"

"Hmm. Yes." Pam responded politely, but her mind was on another strong personality—a contemporary one.

"Here we are!" Wendy called as they pulled into a nearly full parking lot. "Bible study is first, church after. My father is preaching today as well as leading the study. He's so anxious to meet you."

Pam followed her new friend to empty seats in a big room. People were filing in through several doors. Soon Wendy's father came to his feet and began to clear his throat.

"Good morning! It's so nice to see you all here today! We've got a very exciting study planned on Simon Peter, "The Rock." Today I'd like to introduce him to you and tell you a bit about the man he was."

Pam opened her notebook and poised her pen.

"Scripture shows us a vigorous individual in Peter,

48

quick to take initiative. For example, in Matthew fourteen, he's the disciple who volunteers to come to Jesus upon the water. And later in Matthew, he's the one who asks Jesus how many times he must forgive his brothers. Always thinking, always doing, that's Peter.''

Wendy nudged Pam. "I'd never thought of him quite like that. Had you?''

Pam shook her head. It was difficult to think of history's men in today's terms. To think of them as similar to the men she knew—like Ty Evans.

Reverend Williamson continued. "Peter's prominent role among his peers is reflected when he is singled out and the other disciples are mentioned as a group associated with him. It is commonly thought that when the disciples spoke or acted, Peter was normally their spokesman and took the lead. Peter was the one who rallied the disciples after Jesus' arrest had scattered them. He was truly a leader of men. Try to imagine someone you know today who might have some of Peter's personality traits. Our goal in this class is to see Peter the man. Seeing his weaknesses as well as his strengths should give us encouragement. Peter was weak as well as strong; human, not divine. If God can work through Peter, he can work through us as well!''

Heartened by the words, Pam relished the rest of her day. As weak as she felt sometimes, she was reassured she had a Source of power to tap. If only Ty would understand that.

Ty. As she spent a quiet afternoon in her apartment writing letters and putting the finishing touches on her first article, her mind kept turning to him. Disapproving as she was of his forwardness, she felt glimmers of new feelings as well. But until he could understand and accept her faith, those newly aroused emotions had to be kept under wraps. The turmoil in her mind kept her tossing and turning until it was nearly time to rise and get ready for her first day at work.

"Good morning, Miss Warren! Is your first assignment complete?" Pam's boss, Ed Raferty, peered at her over the top of his paper-stacked desk.

"Here it is, sir. I hope it's what you had in mind." Pam thrust the sheets into his meaty hand. Her own fist was shaking too much to hang on to them any longer.

"Well, I apologize for the unexpected assignment. Everyone was calling in sick when you stopped by. I know it wasn't quite proper to send you off on an assignment so unprepared—and not yet on payroll—but we'll make up for it somehow." He chewed a bit on the cigar in his mouth and glanced at the typewritten page, forgetting Pam.

Several moments later he looked up to see her still standing there, waiting for instructions. "Miss Warren, I find this incredible."

Pam's heart sank. He hated it. Her idea of a "scoop" had failed miserably.

"I'm sorry, Sir. But I didn't have much time to get any background material on Mr. Evans. It was the only angle I could think of on such short notice. Do you want me to rewrite it?"

"Rewrite it? Nonsense. It's perfect! It's the most personal story we've ever managed to get on Tiger Evans. He's as elusive as they come. What a headline this will make, 'Tiger Evans—Good Samaritan.' We've been printing the same old stuff for seven years about Evans—how good a hockey player he is, his college degrees, home-town boy made good—that stuff. But there's never any sign that he's human, got a life outside of hockey. When an interviewer goes to talk to him he freezes. At least this is different, a reporter's story of how Evans helped her out. We can offer all those adoring fans a peek into his private life, albeit a small one. Good job, Warren."

Pam's eyes grew as large as moons as she listened. She hadn't realized just how effective Ty's defenses were. And he had let her inside them. She was very flattered.

"By the way, Warren. Your desk is at the back of the room. The one with the big green manual typewriter. A couple more stories like this and we'll find you an electric. And here's your assignment for tomorrow. You don't have to check in if you don't want to. Just get the research done and have it on my desk by eight AM on Wednesday."

Pam was summarily dismissed and wandered dazedly to her desk. She had been given a feature assignment on the strength of that one interview with Ty. Things certainly happened quickly up here. Perhaps Ty's actions were just keeping pace with everything else happening in her life!

By the end of the day, most of it spent in the newspaper's library, the "morgue," Pam had almost forgiven Ty for his boldness. Perversely, she was beginning to regret putting him off. As she studied old files covering her current assignment, she wondered what it would be like to have those thick, strong arms wrapped around her again. She even began to giggle, remembering her first sight of him in the Blazers locker room, purposefully dropping his equipment in front of her, daring her to blush.

Closing her eyes, she could still conjure up the image of that golden furred chest and slim waist . . .

"Miss Warren, are you all right?" A voice broke into the pleasant memories.

Pam opened her eyes to meet a slim young man in tortoise-shell glasses. "Oh, fine. Thank you. I was just, uh, thinking."

"I thought perhaps you didn't feel well. Oh, excuse me, I'm Wendell Adams. I work in Advertising. I saw you with Wendy at church yesterday, but didn't get the opportunity to say hello."

"Hello, Wendell. Nice to meet you." Pam extended a hand in greeting. Here was a man more like those she had known at home. Polite, a bit shy, and, if she dared admit it to herself, probably boring.

Wendell returned his slipping glasses to the bridge of his nose with his index finger and stood there, finger on the nosepiece, thinking. Finally, he spoke. "Miss Warren, I know you don't know me very well, but I'm an acquaintance of Reverend Williamson, and he can vouch for me. Well, what I'm getting at is, I mean would you mind if, only if you'd like to—"

"Yes, Wendell, what *are* you getting at?" Uncharacteristically impatient, Pam found herself tapping a toe. Wendell Adams reminded her very much of the young men her father always encouraged her to date.

"Would you like to go out for supper with me tonight, Miss Warren? I'd be very honored."

Pam hoped he didn't notice her jaw go slack with amazement. Her third dinner invitation in three days! Fighting back the wish that it was Ty instead of the fidgety Wendell who had asked her, Pam nodded evenly.

"Thank you, Wendell. That would be very nice. I do want to be home early, however. I have several letters to write to my family."

"Oh! Of course! I wouldn't dream of keeping you out late on a work night, Miss Warren. Shall we say six-thirty?"

Pam nodded as she jotted down her apartment address. Clutching the scrap of paper like it was divine writ, Wendell backed away alternately smiling and grimacing as he bumped into sharp-cornered desks on his backward trek.

As soon as the slim young man was out of sight, Pam released the bubble of laughter that had been building in her throat. Her father would be delighted with the polite young man, she was sure. Two weeks ago she might have been herself, but after a weekend around Tiger Evans, Wendell Adams seemed dull in comparison.

Shrugging off the moment, Pam turned to her research. The weekend had been fun, but it was obvious from last evening that she and Ty were on different wavelengths. What Ty expected from a woman, she wouldn't give, not outside the bonds of marriage. And Ty Evans didn't seem the marrying kind.

By six-thirty that evening, Pam was in the throes of self-doubt. Wendy had assured her that Wendell was a wonderful man, one of which her father would readily approve. The burning desire for independence that had led her to Winnipeg seemed to chafe at the thought of one more man of her father's choosing. Pamela dearly loved her parents, but felt forced to escape their suffocating overprotection that seemed even to span the miles to Canada.

But even more distressing had been the odd note in Wendy's tone. "Oh, Pam! Wendell Adams? He's such a nice man. And he asked you out? You're so lucky!" The effusive gush came with a restrained sentiment. Pam suspected that there was more than a little envy in Wendy's tone. Wendell Adams had been going to Wendy's church for a long time, and now Pam, the newcomer upstart, was enticing away the desirable Mr. Adams.

Saddened because she hated to hurt her one and only friend in the city, Pam vowed that this would be her first and last date with Wendell. Perhaps she could play matchmaker and remove that hurt tone from her friend's voice.

Cheered by the thought of bringing Wendy and Wendell together, Pam bustled to get her coat. She would plant the seeds tonight, talking about her friend.

The doorbell rang and Wendell Adams stood at the threshold. At least Pam *thought* it was Wendell. The visitor, garbed from neck to ankle in a gray woolen overcoat, had a red muffler wrapped round and round his neck and face until all that showed from beneath a navy-blue stocking cap was a pair of tortoise-shell glasses with frosty lenses.

"Hello, Pamela. Are you ready to go?" The voice sounded vaguely familiar, a little like that of her co-worker—if he were trapped at the bottom of a deep well.

"Wendell? Is that you?" Pam peered into the tiny round spot on each lens of his glasses that had defrosted. Pale blue eyes gleamed back.

"Yes. It's very cold out tonight. Dress warmly." He stood like a stuffed display in her doorway, making no move to enter.

Pam buttoned her coat and edged into the hallway around the immobile Wendell. Wondering wildly for a moment if he had frozen to the spot, she began to regret not slipping on her long underwear. If the weather could do this to a man as well dressed as Wendell, she would never last in the wind's onslaught in a light wool skirt.

"Do you mind if we eat uptown?" the mummified visitor inquired. "I found a parking spot with a headbolt heater, and I hate to move the car. The hotel down the street has a nice restaurant and there are several movie theaters nearby."

Pam nodded agreeably. She was beginning not to trust cars in this bitter cold. They never seemed to start when you wanted them to—except for Ty. He seemed able to warm the engine with a touch of the ignition.

They trudged down the street, wind whipping at their ankles, to the first available doorway.

"Wendell, let's go in here. I don't think I can walk any farther!" Pam yelled across the gusting wind.

The mummy nodded and pulled open the door on a warm and fragrant pizza place.

"It smells good in here. Is this okay with you Pam?" he inquired, lifting the foggy glasses to study her face.

"Just fine. It's warm, and that's all that matters right now. And I love pizza."

"Good." Wendell unwound several feet of muffler from his neck and face. Pam stifled a giggle.

"I see a booth over there. Let's grab it. Everyone seems to have stopped here to eat." Pam pointed to a red leather enclave.

They spent the evening huddled there, never really warming after the winter rawness outside. Pam sipped hot cider with cinnamon stick stirrers until she thought she would explode, but the chill never left her legs and ankles.

"Well, would you like to go to a movie?" Wendell inquired.

"Thank you for offering, but I really think I should be getting home. I have those letters to write and some unpacking to do. I'm rather unsettled yet." And she continued to herself, "I want to stick my feet in a tub of warm water and unthaw them!"

"Whatever you want. Thank you for coming." Wendell said.

"Wendell, how well do you know Wendy?" Pam inquired, her plan not forgotten.

"Uh, not very well. She seems rather quiet."

"Probably tongue-tied around you," Pam thought to herself. Aloud she said, "She's been very good to me since I came to Winnipeg. She's a very nice girl. Perhaps someday you and she could come to my place for dinner. I think you'd like her once you got to know her."

Wendell's pale eyes brightened at the thought. "That would be just fine. I'd like that."

Pam smiled to herself. She had found a way to

repay her friend's kindness. Then she said, "Well, I suppose we'd better bundle up and start back."

The wind was at their backs on the way home, but Pam's teeth would not stop chattering as they rode the elevator to her apartment. Her heart began to pound as rapidly as the click of her molars as she saw a note wedged in her apartment door.

Pulling the paper from the door, she flicked it open: "Pam—Where are you on a night like this? Sorry I missed you. Tiger."

She barely heard Wendell's goodbyes as she stood studying the crumpled sheet. She walked slowly into the apartment with a dejected slump to her shoulders. Missing Ty troubled her more than she had expected. Morosely, she pulled off her clothes and slipped on a fleecy white turtleneck robe and slippers. Then, notepad and pen in hand, she dragged a heating pad and two blankets to the living room couch and padded a warm little nest in one corner. Just as she had herself arranged in a cocoon of blankets, her feet ensconced on the heating pad, her doorbell rang.

Curiosity won over the desire to stay under the quilts, and she shuffled to the door. A warming sight met her on the other side of the peekhole.

"Ty! I thought I'd missed you!" She threw open the door so it shuddered against the wall behind it.

"You did. But I thought I'd give you another chance." He came breezing into the apartment with his coat flapping open, hands in his pockets, apparently oblivious to what the weather was whipping up outside. "You've got to get a phone. I'm not going to make a habit of swinging by here to see if you've frozen up. I'd rather be able to call."

He swept his coat off and tossed it to the floor. Then he stood studying her, his sturdy legs splayed, his arms crossed over his chest. He was wearing stone-washed denims and a rusty wool turtleneck that curled under his chin. Over the sweater he wore a tweedy jacket with leather arm patches the color of his sweater.

The studiously casual attire must have cost a small fortune, Pam thought to herself as she gazed at the welcome sight. Ty seems so sturdy and real when compared with Wendell's aesthetic demeanor. Ty was earthy and strong—and welcome.

"You must be in for the night," he commented, eyeing the nest of blankets on the couch.

"I just about froze earlier, and I can't get warm. Tonight was no night for a walk."

"You *walked* tonight? What in the world for?" Ty flopped into the single tufted chair.

"A young man from work asked me out for dinner. He didn't want to move his car anymore as he had a place to plug it in."

"Humph!" Ty gave a derisive snort before he added, "Sounds like a real winner to me."

"Wendell is very nice. I didn't blame him a bit for not wanting to move the car!" Pam defended.

"Wendell, huh? Well, Wendell sounds like a real charmer." Ty retorted.

"Don't you go criticizing my friends, Tyler Evans. You don't have the right!" Pam suddenly realized the conversation was escalating to unnecessary proportions.

"Aren't I your friend?"

Suddenly it dawned on her that Tyler Evans didn't care about her having dinner with another man. A warm glow began to build in the pit of her stomach, warming her like none of the blankets had done. She smiled slightly as she curled herself back into the cocoon she had built on the couch.

"You are."

"Good. Then let's not talk about this creep Winston anymore."

"Wendell."

"I thought we weren't going to talk about Wentworth anymore."

"Okay. We won't talk about *Wendell* any more."
They were both smiling now, and Ty had left his perch
on the chair to sit on the couch nearer her feet.

"Are you really cold?" he asked with concern.
Unconsciously he was rubbing her toes under the
blankets.

"I seem to get chilled to the very core. Even when
my skin warms up I still feel cold inside."

"You just aren't acclimated yet. I've got the very
thing to warm up your insides. You don't happen to
have any brandy do you?"

Pam shot him a daggered look. "You know I don't,
Ty. Why do you ask?"

"I dunno. Just thought my bad influence might have
started to rub off on you already. How about honey
and lemons. Do you have those?"

"That I have. Honey is in the cupboard, lemons in
the fridge."

"Good enough. I'll be right back." Ty sauntered
into the kitchen and Pam could hear the clatter of a
pan on the stove and the sounds of running water.
Soon doors opened and closed. Finally Ty must have
found what he was looking for because everything
quieted, and he came into the room carrying two
steaming mugs on a tray.

"Here you are. Hot lemonade and honey with a
cinnamon stick swizzle. Guaranteed to warm up those
icy insides." He set the tray on the coffee table and
handed a mug to Pam. She wrapped her fingers
around the heated cup and inhaled the perfumy
vapors.

"Umm. Smells wonderful."

Ty settled himself in the corner of the couch and
unconsciously Pam stretched out her legs until her
feet rested on his thigh. Between his presence and the
lemonade she was warm for the first time all day. He
seemed comfortable with the silence and they sat
there in domestic companionship.

Pam awoke as her head jerked upward with a start. She had dozed off soundly. Her embarrassed gaze met Ty's amused one. He had been watching her sleep. A darting glance to the wall clock made her gasp.

"Ty! It's three o'clock in the morning! Why didn't you wake me?"

"I was enjoying the view. Are you warm now?"

Warmer than she had ever been before. Deep down inside she felt warm in places she barely knew existed.

But some of her warmth was departing. Ty stood to leave.

"Well, Miss Priss. It's been wonderful spending the night with you, but I'd better leave. Now that you're awake, it might be harder to be a gentleman. Do you have any free time tomorrow?"

Pam smiled and stretched. "Most of the day, actually. I'm doing a feature. The ground work is done. I have the interview at nine and don't have to have it in until Wednesday morning."

"Then can you spend the day with me?"

"What about your practice?"

"We're going from six AM until ten tomorrow. Something about a coaches clinic somewhere in the city."

"Ty! You have to be at practice in three hours?"

"Nothing to it. I'm used to short nights and long days. Actually this was pretty restful. I would have fallen asleep myself if it hadn't been for the view." He squeezed her big toe. "G'night, Miss Priss. See you before noon."

He threw the big coat over his shoulder and strolled to the door. "I've locked it. Just curl up where you are and go back to sleep." With that he pulled the door shut behind him.

Pam stood for a moment, catching a glimpse of herself in the mirror over the couch. Her blond curls cascaded across her shoulders, and her brown eyes were tender with unspoken emotion. Her cheeks, rosy from sleep, looked soft and dewy. Yawning lazily, she dropped back to the couch and curled under the covers, her toes searching out the warmed spot on the couch Ty had just vacated.

So last night was not the only side of Tyler Evans. He could be as gentlemanly and understanding as he could be demanding. Finally warmed, Pam curled into a ball and fell asleep.

CHAPTER 4

"GOOD MORNING. MISS PRISS! Are you warmer today?"
Ty greeted her laughingly at her door. He looked
rested and chipper, a seemingly impossible feat on
less than three hours of sleep. He wore black slacks
and sweater and a fur-lined black-leather jacket that
was turned up at the collar shielding the lower portion
of his face. A black-leather cap with visor was
perched jauntily over his honeyed curls and tilted
slightly over his right eye. Ty kept his right side to the
hallway and leaned back against the door waiting for
Pamela to get her coat.

Pam smiled inwardly. The hour she had devoted to
primping seemed worth it all now. She had spent time
before the mirror practicing with the make-up she so
seldom wore. She would need make-up that morning
to counteract the unfeminine feeling of long johns
swathing her legs and arms under her clothing. She
had finally warmed up and wasn't about to be chilled
again.

Ty seemed to be watching her closely. His face was
still turned slightly away from her and only after she

had her coat about her did she think his pose slightly unusual.

"Ty, is something wrong? Why are you looking at me that way? Ty! What happened?"

He purposefully turned toward her then to give her a full view of his face. Most of the right side was blackened across the eye and cheek. Angry red streaks shot through the bruise. Ty shrugged nonchalantly.

"No big deal. Got hit in the head. Still want to go out with me, looking like a war victim?"

"You got hit in the head? Why aren't you at a hospital? How did it happen? What . . ." Pam reached to touch the wicked bruise, but Ty winced and backed away.

"I've been poked and prodded quite enough today, thank you. I'm fine. No concussion. No broken bones. Nothing. Doctor said I was lucky to get hit in the head. Any place else and I might have hurt something."

Pam pulled him into the apartment and forced him to the couch. Standing above him, feet spread, hands on her hips, she started her inquisition.

"All right. What happened?"

"I got hit with a stick at practice. Can we go now?"

"No. Why didn't your helmet protect you?"

"I wasn't wearing it. Can we go now?"

"Why weren't you wearing it?"

"Didn't feel like it. Don't make a big deal of this, Pam. Can we go now, or are you ashamed to be seen with me?"

"I'd never be ashamed of you, Ty, but this scares me. What if you'd been seriously injured? You told me you always wore a helmet!"

"Pam, I've been battered around all the years I've been playing hockey. This is just a scratch. I always do wear my helmet for the games. Not all the guys even do that. Relax!"

She felt tears prickling at the back of her eyes and an old terror rising in her throat. Was everything dangerous in the lives of the men she admired?

"Pam, are you trembling?" Ty took her shoulders and shook her gently. "I'm just fine. I only look terrible. Really!"

"Did you go to a reputable doctor?" Pam inquired tearily.

"The team doctor is one of the best. They even sent me to the team dentist. No teeth even loose. Three or four days and you'll hardly notice the bruise."

Ty stepped back in surprise as Pam vented her anger, "And what kind of a game is it that every team needs its own doctor and dentist! It's so unsafe, Ty, why do you play it?"

"I like it. And it's not all that dangerous. I'm sorry I didn't wear a helmet this morning. Then when I took the blow all I'd have is ringing ears. I promise I won't play without it again. Just calm down!" He had her by the shoulders but the trembling wouldn't subside. She stood in his arms shaking. Rivulets flowed from her dark eyes down her cheeks and into the scarf at her neck.

"Pam, what's causing all this commotion?" Ty shook her gently. "You can't be that upset about a black eye!"

Visions of a race car track and a billow of black smoke pirouetted in her brain. Pam breathed deeply before responding. "You're right, Ty. But I can't talk about it now. I'm glad you're safe. Maybe you'd better get me out of here and show me the town. And prove to me that you didn't get your brains knocked loose with that blow."

Ty grinned and then winced at the pain in his cheek. "I don't know what makes you tick, Pam, but I'm sure it's complicated. Come on."

Pam forgot about Ty's near-miss as they toured the Manitoba Museum. He was as enthused and childlike as the eight-year-old with the family ahead of them. He grabbed her hand and pulled her along from one display to the next before she had time to read any of the descriptions.

"Come on. Let's go see the dinosaurs. They're right on the way to the ship."

"What ship, Ty? You're pulling me so fast I can't stop and study it all."

"You can't see it all in one visit. I've been coming here for years. We've got a lot to do today. This is the overview. We'll come back and spend the day sometime if you want to read everything."

We'll come back someday . . . The words had a magical permanence to Pam's ears. Every time Ty appeared on her doorstep she was afraid it would be the last. He was too much like his nickname—a wild untamable jungle creature. He would hate the confines she knew she would demand of him. They were too different. Poles apart on the things that mattered most.

"Here's the ship, Pam. What do you think?" Ty's voice broke into her musings. Before her *was* a ship, life-sized and real, docked in a fantasy village and open for tours.

"This is wonderful!" Pam squealed and headed for the boarding ramp. For the next hour they were lost to the world exploring Canadian history.

"Well, where do we go from here?" Pam inquired gazing back over her shoulder at the museum exit.

"Are you hungry?"

"Only a little. What time is it?"

"Two o'clock. Let's stop and get a hamburger on the way to the zoo."

"The zoo? Ty, it's December and freezing! Whatever is there to see at the zoo?"

"There are some animals that like it cold, remember? Did you ever hear of polar bears in Arizona?"

"Very funny. The point is, *I'm* no polar bear. I want to be warm!"

"There are warming enclosures at the zoo. We can even have coffee out there if you like. Come on. You might be surprised."

Everything Ty did was a surprise, Pam decided, munching on a hamburger in his car on the way to the zoo. He was intense one minute, playful the next. He was open and charming as long as her life was under discussion, closed and distant when anything related to his arose.

He was obviously a local boy. That was apparent by his familiarity with the city and its subtle nuances. But he might have sprung from some hockey arena unparented for all he spoke of his family. Only the magnificent fur coats he wore hinted that he might have some relationship with his father the furrier. The distant look that came into his eyes when Pam's questions became too probing kept her from persisting.

"Here we are. Are you done with that food?"

"All but the fries. Want some?"

"Chips."

"What?" Pam glanced at him, puzzled.

"Not fries. Chips. That's what you'll have to start calling them now."

"How British!"

"It's our heritage, you know. It goes with the territory. You'll also have to quit saying 'about' with an 'ow' sound in it and start saying 'aboot,' as in, 'It's aboot time to go and see the zoo.'" Ty was grinning widely. Pam loved the soft inflections of his voice. His words often seemed like a caress, they were so soft and melodic.

"I agree. It's 'aboot' time. Let's go."

Snow crunched noisily under their shoes as they entered the zoo's metal gates. Ty steered her toward the bears. No grizzlies were apparent, but two black bears were sunning in the weak midday rays. Nearby the polar bears romped in the snow, rolling and batting at each other like big kittens.

"Let's go over here. There's an animal you might not have seen before." Ty took Pam's elbow and steered her toward another cage.

"What are they?" Pam stared at the reddish-brown doglike animals.

"Kiangsi Dholes. Like a wild dog. They're related to the hyena. There are more here than anywhere else in the world except China."

"You certainly seem to know a lot about this zoo," Pam commented.

"Years of experience. I spent many weekends a year out here while I was growing up."

Pam waited expectantly, hoping Ty would reveal more of himself, but he seemed to realize his tongue had loosened and his jaw clamped shut, and they walked on in silence.

"Look at that bird! It looks like it's wearing pantaloons!"

Ty's eyes followed Pam's finger to a snowy owl on a perch. "And what do you know about pantaloons, Miss Priss? Is that a usual part of your wardrobe?"

"Very funny," she commented dryly, blushing a little as she thought of the thermal underwear she was wearing, not so dissimilar in function to the fluffy feathers on the little bird's legs.

"Cold yet?" Ty inquired.

"A little. Is there a place to warm up?"

"We'll go to the monkey house. I could stand in there for hours, and it's plenty warm."

By the time Pam was warm, Ty had taken off his coat and hat. It had been some hours since she had consciously thought of the bruise on his cheek and again it sent a darting bolt of fear through her.

"What's on your mind, Miss Priss? You look like you've seen a ghost," Ty inquired at the anguished look on her face.

"I was just looking at your cheek."

"My mug isn't that ugly, is it?"

"You know what I mean. Does it hurt?"

"Nah. Only when I smile. But then again, you've been making me smile quite a bit today."

"I'm sorry."

"You are? I'm not. I'm having a great time. I haven't been to any of these places in ages. I feel like a tourist. Come on. Forget about the bruise. Let's go look at the cats."

"What kind of cats would want to be out in this weather?" Pam scoffed.

"The kind that come from Siberia. They think this is summer. And there are some snow leopards too. This is their favorite season."

By the time they had looked at the lynx, leopards, and Siberian tigers, Pam was shivering again. Ty looked down at her and shook his head. "You worry me. You've got to get acclimated. Let's go into the Tropical House and warm up. Do you like birds?"

"They're in cages, I hope?" Pam asked unsteadily. Birds struck more fear into her heart than any mouse or snake ever could. She leaned heavily against Ty's arm as they entered the steamy, summerlike domed building. A small bird dive-bombed past her head, and she shuddered.

"Ty, I don't like it here. I'm scared of birds."

The air was split with trilling and whistling and the rackety caw of some unidentified resident. Pam stepped backward and nearly fell into a pit containing three large, sleepy turtles.

Her scream blended with that of a macaw blaring from a tree limb. She felt Ty's arms around her, pulling her upward. She clung to him, quivering, drawing strength from the strong warm body.

"It's okay, honey. It's all right." She could hear Ty whispering softly in her ear. A tear squeezed from beneath each tightly closed lid and drizzled down her cheeks. "Come on. I think you're better off outside in the cold than in here with the birds." He led her docilely to the door. She stood, still shaking, while he buttoned the front of her coat and tugged the stocking cap over her curls.

She came to her senses as his hands, unaccustomed to such maneuvers, pulled the folded brim of her knit hat over onto her nose, blinding her.

"Whoa!" She folded the band upward, exposing the laughter in her dark eyes. "I may be scared of birds, but now that we're out of that room, you don't have to cover my eyes!"

"Sorry. Are you okay? I've never seen anyone react to a bird like that." Ty's golden eyes were wide with concern.

"It's silly, I know. But I can't seem to help it. Brr." She shuddered in revulsion. "They're such icky things—spikey, feathery wings, scaled legs like little dinosaurs, bug eaters—"

"Stop it before I begin hating them myself! Come on. We'll walk by the elk and bison on the way out. They're nice and earth-bound."

Ty threw his arm around Pam's shoulders as they strolled toward the exit. She didn't resist the comforting hollow of his arm. It seemed so right to have him there, protective, concerned. How quickly she had fallen prey to his charm! As long as she didn't think of the angry bruise on his cheek and how he got it or of his flippant attitude toward things spiritual, she could relax and enjoy his company.

But the shadows that hovered over him were growing. And no matter how violently she resisted her thoughts, she knew Ty Evans could never be hers.

"Well, how about it? Aren't you going to answer me?"

Pamela's head snapped up. "What did you say? I was thinking about something."

"Obviously. You were a million miles away. In Arizona, maybe?" Ty had a curious light in his eyes.

"Oh, farther than that. But now I'm back. What did you ask me?"

"If you wanted to go ice skating."

"Ice skating? Don't you ever get tired of ice skating?"

"No I haven't yet. When I do, I'll quit. Want to go?"

"Ty, I don't know how to skate. I'd break my neck."

"Not with me to teach you. I'm the big hockey star, remember? I'll teach you to skate like I do."

Pam remembered him gliding down the ice with consummate ease—and diving into a vicious fight at the net with his teammates.

"I'm not sure I could survive the kind of skating you do," she commented dryly.

"Trust me. I started skating when I was two. It will be a breeze."

"Two years old? Ty, you were just a baby! Who taught you?"

The icy wind was suddenly no more chilly than Ty's tone. "My father."

This mysterious father loomed like a vision without a face in Pam's mind. Whoever or whatever he was, he had at least taught his tiny son to skate—and given him a dream to fulfill. Wisely, Pam changed her tactics.

"I don't have any skates, Ty. Sorry." She was suddenly relieved to have never owned such contraptions.

"Then I'll buy you some. Come on. I know exactly what you need."

"I can't accept a gift from you, Ty. You've done too much already."

"Let me buy you skates. It will please me, Prudish Pamela. After all, skating is my life."

"Ty, I just can't—"

"Sure you can. Please? It will be a Christmas present. For both of us."

She found herself weakening. He seemed to want her to have them very badly.

"A Christmas present?"

"Yup. An early one. You're gonna love it."

Within minutes Pamela found her feet being stuffed into gleaming white skates with polished silver blades.

"I think you'll find figure skates easier for you, Pam," Ty was busy explaining as he tied the skates on her feet. The clerk, in awe of Ty's presence in the store, stood back and gaped at his hero. "These little ridges at the tip," and Ty ran his fingers across the serrated toe picks, "will help you to stop. Hockey skates don't have those and you have to turn your foot to the side to stop. I think these should work for you. There. How do they fit?"

"They hurt my ankles, Ty!"

"That's because they're a little stiff. Maybe I laced them too tightly. You need plenty of support, though. I can see by the way your ankles are wobbling."

Pam was standing upright on the thin blades, teetering precariously. "Should I be standing up in them?" she asked.

Ty laughed. "It's better than falling down. You have to walk to the ice in them, you know. Anyway, these blades aren't sharpened." To the gawking clerk he added, "We'll take these. Sharpen them, please."

By the time Pamela had her boots and outer clothing back in place, Ty had the skates under his arm. The more eager he was to get to the ice, the more reluctant Pam began to feel. She had made a fool of herself once today, in the bird house. Twice would be ridiculous.

"Here we are. This is where I learned to skate." Ty tugged her toward a low-slung indoor arena. Small children stopped to gape when they saw Tiger Evans carrying two sets of skates to the ice. Ty pushed Pam back onto a bench in the warming room and proceeded to undo her boots and put on her skates. The thought flickered through Pamela's mind that this was the most intimate and personal thing she had ever let a man do for her. He had the blade of her skate and part of her foot between his knees to lace the boot.

His head, bent low over his work, was very near her face, and she could smell the scent of clean hair and tangy lime. The sensation made her slightly giddy.

"There!" He dropped her foot to the ground and looked at her expectantly. "You're ready to skate." In a fraction of the time he had taken with her he had his own skates on and was standing with hand outstretched waiting for her.

Biding for time, Pamela inquired, "Do you always carry a pair of skates in your trunk?"

"Sometimes two or three. You can never have too many pairs of skates, you know. Now what are you stalling for? It's time for your first lesson!" Ty looked very secure on the thin silver blades. Surely it couldn't be that difficult, Pam decided.

Unwillingly she stood and tottered toward him, feeling very insecure. She had never realized that being two inches off the ground could feel so dangerous.

"That-a-girl!" Ty cheered, obviously squelching a grin.

Pam's ankles felt watery and she leaned forward and grasped the hand Ty offered. "And you play games on these things!"

"Come on, Miss Athlete, and show me what you can do." He half pulled and half carried her to the ice.

"Ty, I can't do this. I just can't." Pam felt the world sliding from under her feet.

"Sure you can. But you're going to have to let go of my arm. I think you've stopped the circulation. If I took my glove off, I'm sure I'd find my fingers blue. Just hold onto my hands lightly. I'll skate backward and pull you along."

"Backward? So I can look you in the eye when I

fall down and break my leg?'' She clutched wildly at his arms.

"Don't fight me, Pam. Just relax. Otherwise you'll pull us both over." Ty weaved back and forth, pulling her along with him.

With her teeth gritted and eyes squeezed tight, Pam's primary sensation was the breeze filtering through her hair. She had not realized how fast they were going until she opened her eyes and saw sections of the arena sidewalls flash by. With a terrified screech, she tried to grab for Ty's midsection, no longer feeling safe extended from the end of his arms.

As she lunged, she fell. Her feet went out from under her and she slid unceremoniously between Ty's legs on the ice. To avoid her, he twisted sharply, lifting one leg over her. Putting one hand on the ice to steady himself, he skated a half circle around her before catching his balance.

"All right, Lady. You almost took me over with you . . . whoa!" Still in a panic and unable to get to her feet, Pamela grabbed at Ty's pant leg and pulled him undecorously on top of her on the ice.

Mortified, she finally lay still when she heard a voice carrying across the rink, "Hey! That lady pulled Ty Evans over on top of her! First time I ever saw Tiger go down like that!"

"Now you did it." His voice was near her ear, and his weight was crushing across her body, but he made no move to alter his position.

"Ty, get off me."

"You've ruined my reputation at the rink where I grew up. Now what am I going to do?" Still he did not budge.

"I'm sorry, Ty. I'm just never going to be a skate—" Her sentence remained unfinished as his lips came over hers, and she felt her head pressing back against the ice. The next thing she was cognizant of was a delighted peal of laughter from one of the many spectators who had gathered to see their fallen hero.

"At least he knows how to make the best of a bad situation!"

"I know he'd never do that in a game."

"There's nobody that good looking at the games."

The bandying continued, and finally Ty rolled sideways, releasing Pam. Ty stood up with no difficulty, but it took all of his strength to pull the recumbent Pamela from the ice. Sticking a supporting arm beneath her armpit and winking at the gathering crowd, he slid her from the ice, insuring that she would not tumble again.

"I think I'm going to die." Pamela mumbled once inside the warming room.

"Are you hurt?" Ty's golden gaze was wide and serious.

"Only my pride. But I think it's terminal. How embarrassing."

"What about me? I'm the big hockey star. How do you think it looked for me to be sprawled out there on you—I mean on the ice?" Ty couldn't keep the laughter from his voice.

"You made the best of a difficult situation, I noticed," Pam commented wryly, pulling at her skates.

"Let me do that for you. I'll feel safer once you're back in boots. Maybe there *are* people that can't learn to skate." Ty's cheerful attitude did nothing for her self-confidence.

"It's a rare breed, but I think a good share of them come from Arizona. Ow!"

"What? Is it your ankle?" Ty pulled the woolen sock from her foot and his fingers gently explored the soft hollows of her ankle.

"I just twisted it on the way down. I'm not a graceful faller either."

"It's starting to swell. Let's get you back to my place and put some ice on it."

"I shouldn't, Ty, really. I'll just go soak it at home."

"We're twenty minutes closer to my house. And anyway," he looked at her steadily, "isn't the newspaper reporter in you curious to see where I live?"

He had hit a familiar chord. More and more Pam wanted to learn about Tiger Evans. Now the opportunity was presenting itself. And her ankle was beginning to throb.

"Just for the ice, then," she finally consented.

"Did I ever mention anything else?" he countered. But she could see in his eyes that Tiger Evans had more than her ankle on his mind.

The ankle was throbbing by the time they reached Ty's apartment. Pamela hobbled into the elevator, and with a muted swoosh, they were on the eleventh floor of a very sumptuous apartment complex. At the elevator's threshold Ty swept Pamela off her feet and carried her down the hall. A light, giddy feeling began in her stomach, and nervous butterflies fluttered their wings within her.

Resting in Ty's arms was as secure as the blades of her skates were precarious, and it was with no little regret that they came to his door, and he put her down to dig deep into his pocket for a key.

"Here we are." He swept her up again and carried her to the couch. Vague images of a honeymooning couple came to Pam's mind, and she had a rosy blush on her cheeks as she found herself being unceremoniously dumped to the cushions.

Ty tossed his jacket across a chair and headed for the kitchen. "I'll get an ice pack. It just so happens I have a dozen or two around here. Every time somebody gets banged up they send another one home with 'em. Someday I'll return them all and replenish the supply."

As he clattered in the kitchen, Pam studied her surroundings. The apartment was as bold and handsome as its owner. Unbroken navy blue carpet ran the

74

length of the living room and down the hallway and the kitchen floor was a pristine white tile. The large square room was broken into kitchen, dining and living areas, unfettered by walls. Pam could watch Ty dumping ice into a red rubber ice pack from her perch. The kitchen cupboards were navy blue as well and gleamed with a hard polished patina. Stark white walls enveloped the room.

Bold geometric artwork in navy and white with occasional flashes of red graced Ty's walls. The modern navy and white furniture was all leather and suede. Digging her hands into the cushion of the couch, Pam could feel the velvety softness of an ultra-suede cushion. Ty's living room furniture easily cost more than all of her possessions—including her car. But the room told her very little about its inhabitant.

"Pam you want something to drink? Want a beer—oops!" Ty had a chagrined look on his face. "Sorry, force of habit. Tea. Tea? I'll bet you want tea!" He looked so apologetic and hopeful that Pam laughed aloud. At least he was beginning to learn.

Soon he brought a red ceramic mug of steaming tea and placed it on the glass coffee table before her. The ice pack he clutched under one arm, close to his body.

"There. Now let's take a look at that ankle. Does it hurt?" He settled at her feet and took the throbbing appendage in his hands. Moving slowly he manipulated her foot, testing, probing. "Can you wiggle your toes?"

Pam nodded and did so. Simultaneously she leaned over to reach for her tea.

"You'll be fine. If I told you how many times I pulled, bruised, or strained something you'd wonder why I kept on skating. Just let me massage your ankle for a minute. What's this?"

The hot tea scalded the lining of Pam's throat as it sizzled its way down, but her throat was burned no more than her cheeks as Ty lifted the leg of her pants to reveal the unflattering long johns riding an inch above her ankle.

"Ty Evans, quit that!" Pam tried to jerk her leg away, but he held her fast.

He was grinning impishly and theatrically admiring the little butterflies and flowers above the white ribbing at the ankle. "No wonder you could stand the zoo and skating today! I thought you were getting used to the temperatures. Well, Pamela, I have to give you credit."

"Credit?" she squeaked, embarrassed at her unfeminine attire.

"For being sensible. At least you're warm. But," and he gave a lecherous roll to his eyes, "there *is* more attractive feminine attire, I know."

Not daring to ask how he might know, Pam pulled her leg away. Ty was too disconcerting sometimes.

"Hey! I almost forgot!" He came to his feet in a fluid leap.

"What's wrong?"

"Nothing. I just forgot to pick up my mail when we came in. I haven't read the paper yet today. I heard there was an article in there by my favorite reporter. Interested in seeing it?" He turned and gave her an enigmatic look.

The butterflies returned to Pam's stomach full force. Suddenly she was fearful. Each day she had known him had confirmed more fully his need for privacy. Perhaps she had already stepped over the boundaries he set for others who were close to him. Even after these few days, she feared hurting him. He had let her into his life so willingly when she needed someone most. To betray him would break her heart. But would he consider this story a betrayal?

Ty returned from the door with a stack of letters and the paper in hand. Tossing the letters aside, he opened the paper to the sports page and began to read. Over his shoulder Pam could see the edge of her headline. A three column photo of Ty in his uniform from the paper's morgue was centered over the article.

Her eyes darted from the page to Ty's face and back again. A closed, impassive look shuttered his feelings. Pam sensed that he was as tense as she. For the first time in her brief career, she began to wonder why she had chosen to be a reporter. An interloper. An intruder. Perhaps Ty did not want the image of good Samaritan. Perhaps a part of his awesome appeal was his independent roughness. Perhaps she'd gone too far.

Her fears were confirmed by his words.

"Well, Pamela, you've done it now."

CHAPTER 5

"DID I DO SOMETHING WRONG? Are you angry?" Pamela felt a surge of unprofessional panic at his words. Ty's feelings seemed far more important than the assignment now. Regret gnawed at her.

"Wrong? Wrong! You made me look like a pussy cat! Now how am I going to convince my opponents that I'm a big, tough hockey player?" Ty let the paper drift to the floor and settled himself beside her on the couch. "That nice-guy stuff was just for you, Prudish Pamela."

Relief welled through her at the playful tone of his voice. He wasn't angry after all! Pam didn't even realize that she had given a deep sigh of relief until Ty's silky laughter penetrated her respite.

"Scared you, huh?"

"I just about went into heart failure. I've been worried ever since I handed that thing in that you'd be furious. I didn't know what else to write. You don't give an interviewer many facts, you know."

A cold, shuttered look flickered for a moment in his eyes, but he laughed. "You painted me to look like the nicest guy in Manitoba, Pam. If I'd known how kind the press could be, I might have relinquished some of my secrets earlier.''

''I don't think you've surrendered any secrets yet, Ty. I know as little about you now as I did the day I met you.'' Pam's voice held a hint of reproach.

The protective barriers she had seen so many times in the past days fell into place but Ty kept his voice light, flippant.

''You've eaten in my favorite restaurants; you've skated on my home rink; you've worn your long johns in to my home—Pamela, you probably know more about me than anyone else in Winnipeg!''

''What about your parents, Ty? And your drinking buddies.'' There. She had it out, the troublesome questions were in the open.

''My parents know very little about me, Pamela. They didn't understand me as a child and nothing has changed since I grew up. And as for my 'drinking buddies' as you call them, they don't come here. No one does. Until you.''

A knife twisted in her heart. Ty painted a lonely picture. Success. Fame. Money. Looks. And isolation.

''I'm sorry, Ty. I've said too much. I'm virtually a stranger to you and I've come galumphing into your life with combat boots on, treading in places that I have no business being. Forgive me.''

''There's nothing to forgive, Pamela. You'll just have to accept me as I am. Not open like you. There are things in my life I've chosen not to talk about. Unhappy things, unhealed wounds. You'll have to accept me as I am or not at all. It's up to you.''

''Wounds can be healed, Ty. There is an Ultimate Healer, you know. If you could turn those things over to Him, He could help you.'' Pam spoke cautiously, fearful of turning him away.

''Not these wounds, Pam. Not by your God, not by

79

anyone. But," and he stood up, "I don't think we need to have any more serious discussion today. Don't try and change me, Pam, and I'll not try to change you."

Picking up on the lighter note, Pam responded, "Then you should never have taken me ice skating. That is a life-altering step if I've ever experienced one! My ankle may never be the same."

"Whoa! I almost forgot! I'm glad you mentioned skating! There's a benefit game going on in Toronto, and some of the Blazer's'players are skating in it. They're raising money for some children's hospital. I meant to watch it." He strode toward the large projection screen television on one wall and flipped it on.

"Why aren't you playing in it, Ty?"

"They drew straws to decide who'd go. Everyone volunteered, and it seemed the fairest way. It's fun to visit those little kids after a benefit. They think they're seeing real heros. And they're the heroic ones—being brave in a hospital. Look! There's Brock Madsen. You can always tell Brock. He's the one without the helmet." Ty perched on the edge of a chair and stared intently at the screen.

Pam's eyes followed Ty's form. He *was* a hero, whether he knew it or not. His modesty and self-deprecating humor were part of his charm. No wonder little children were awestruck—she was—and hockey had been a part of her life for less than a week.

"Bad call! Aw! Two minutes for that? What a gyp!" Ty was roaring at the referee.

Pam, still unsure of the nuances of the game, found herself looking at the individual players—what little she could see of them under their gear.

"Ty, what is all that stuff the players wear?"

"Protective gear mostly. The centres, wings, and defensemen all have shin guards, knee and hip pads, elbow and shoulder pads under their shirt and pants.

The goalie wears even more, of course. He wears goal pads, shoulder and arm protectors, and a bodypad as well as a face mask. He's the one they're shooting at, after all."

"What are those things on his hands called?" Pam studied the wide screen as the goalie deflected a puck.

"A stick glove and a catch glove. A 'blocker' and a 'trapper.' I always think a goalie looks like an armadillo by the time he's dressed."

Pam chuckled. There were definite similarities. Just then Brock Madsen skated onto the screen.

"Ty, I still don't understand why he doesn't wear a helmet. One look at the right side of your face should convince him of that." She had pushed that occurrence into the recesses of her mind until now.

"It's his choice, Pam. I agree with you. I wouldn't go into a game without a helmet. But this morning I just wanted to leave it off. And I paid the price."

"What if one day the price is higher than you want to pay?"

"It's the risk you take. No one ever said hockey was a gentle sport."

Obviously edgy at the turn of the conversation, Ty began tapping the toe of his shoe on the carpet. Almost to himself he added, "I've been lucky, Pam. I've got such a good average because I haven't been sidelined with injuries. I won't take any special risks. I'd like to retire from hockey in one piece."

Still troubled, Pam turned back to the television. She had known another man with that same attitude once. And the price he paid for daring was far too costly.

Lost in thought, Pam took her eyes off the screen to gaze at the Winnipeg skyline. It was Ty's sharp intake of breath that brought her eyes back to his face.

He was white as a sheet. Her eyes darted to the screen where cameramen were zeroing in on a prone player on the ice. A helmetless player. Brock Madsen's face came onto the screen in bloody splendor, and Ty gave a sharp oath.

The sports announcer in a frenzied tone reported, "Brock Madsen of the Winnipeg Blazers is down. Madsen, who rarely wears a helmet, has been hit in the head. From what we can see, it may be an eye injury. A doctor has been called to the ice. We will break now for a commercial and return with—"

"Ty, what happened?" Pam gasped.

"He took a stick in the eye. He and another player were going after the puck in the corner, and a stick came up and hit him. Blast! I wonder which hospital they're taking him to."

Ty paced the floor like a wild man, frightening Pam in the process. She had been through this once before—waiting to hear the extent of a man's injuries—and when the news came it had been worse than anyone had expected.

A pall fell over the afternoon. Unconsciously at first, then with more and more realization, Pam began to see Ty in a new manner. The silences. The danger. The risk. Ty lived in a world of shadows. They hovered over him like phantom clouds, poised to strike. Pam shuddered. Could she risk caring for a man again who toyed with such potent trouble? Was Ty strong and sturdy enough to survive those shadowy hazards of his profession?

Once before she had been fond of a man who loved peril—and peril's close companion, car racing. And his passion had killed him.

The afternoon light dimmed and Ty and Pam sat quietly in the oncoming darkness. Finally, Ty spoke.

"I wonder how he's doing. It didn't look good."

"You can't always tell, Ty. Sometimes there's a lot of blood from a tiny scratch. Especially on the head."

He looked at her in disbelief. "Good try, Pam, but I'm no fool. It looked bad. Brock is the fourth friend of mine to be injured this season. It's happening too

82

often. Sometimes it scares me. It really does." He rubbed the back of his neck, kneading the tight muscles and rolling his head from side to side in an effort to relax. He winced each time his movements affected his bruised cheek.

Sensing that he would like to be alone, Pam slid off the couch and gingerly tried her ankle. Gratefully she realized that all was well. As she slipped into her coat she neared Ty. Next to him, she stood and brushed back the dark golden curls that he tousled with anxious fingers.

"I'll go now. I know you need to be alone. Let me know how he is when you hear."

Quietly she departed, leaving Ty alone in the darkness and the shadows that surrounded him.

There was no word from Ty for the rest of the week. Daily Pamela scanned the incoming news articles for word of Brock Madsen. The news was never good. Pam found the reporter covering Madsen at his desk on Saturday morning.

"Hi, Rick. Anything new of Brock Madsen?"

Rick tilted his head sideways and stared at her. "You're mighty interested in his injuries, Pam. Any special reason?"

"Well, not really. I just happened to be watching the game when it happened."

"With Ty Evans, by any chance?"

Pam's blush was answer enough.

"You've become quite friendly with him in the short time you've been in the city. That's quite an accomplishment. I'm surprised Evans has allowed it."

"Allowed it? What do you mean by that?" A knot tightened in her stomach.

"Evans is gun-shy where reporters are concerned. He gives out information like a miser gives out hundred-dollar bills. I should think you'd jeopardize his privacy."

"Ty has been very kind. He started my car for me. That's all. Now, then, how's Madsen?" Pam desperately wanted the conversation to end. All week she had worried that Ty had been more upset over the article than he'd let on.

"Madsen is still in the hospital. I talked with the team physician this morning. All they know for sure is that his retina was damaged in the blow. His visual acuity isn't good, but the eye is still swollen so they can't tell if the blood supply had been severely disrupted. It may end his career. Too bad, too. He was talking retirement in a year or so. Now he's got that to live with."

Pam recalled the look of resignation on Ty's countenance that evening. He was mentally putting himself in Madsen's place and weighing the consequences, she was sure. She knew deep within that he would take the risks just to continue to play.

"Rick, how old are hockey players when they retire?" she inquired.

"Well, it's a young sport. A thirty-five-year-old is a pretty old man in hockey. The Blazers is a younger team than most. Ty Evans is one of the oldest and he's only twenty-eight. I hope this doesn't make him think about retirement. The team would be lost without him."

"Is he really that good?"

"Yeh. He really is. He's a top scorer, versatile, a fan favorite. But more important than that, he's what's kept the team together and winning on more than one occasion."

"What do you mean, Rick?" Pam perched on the edge of his desk, intrigued.

"Ty's a real leader. The Blazers have come close to defeat more than once, and Ty has rallied them. I've heard him giving pep talks to the guys, and it works, every time. Once after a loss, I was in the locker room, and he was giving them a speech about bouncing back that made me want to stand up and salute. Quite a guy, that Tiger. It really makes you wonder what his background is like." Rick shook his head in awe.

"But surely *someone* knows about it! How can a man grow up in a city and not have someone remember him as a child!"

"Oh, people do. His father is a big furrier here. But he doesn't talk about Ty any more than Ty talks about him. It's like they're not related. I don't think I've ever seen either of his parents at a game. No, I'd say Ty's pretty much alone. By choice, of course. He could have a different woman every night if he wanted to." Suddenly Rick saw the distressed look on Pam's features and stopped rambling. "Ah, but that doesn't mean he does, Pam. Don't get me wrong. If Ty has any romances, they're kept as quiet as the rest of his life."

"Thanks, Rick, for filling me in." The rest of the day and all that night Tiger Evans roamed about Pam's thoughts and dreams, keeping tranquillity at bay.

She woke Sunday morning feeling as unrested as when she had gone to bed, but Pam pulled herself from beneath the covers and dressed for church. She was waiting at the door when Wendy arrived to pick her up.

"Hi, Wendy! How have you been all week?"

"Just fine. And you must be too. I expected you to call if you needed anything."

"The phone was installed on Friday, and I've been so busy at work, I've hardly had time to think. I've only written to my family once since I arrived. Soon they will think I've been swallowed up in the wilds of Canada!"

Wendy laughed. "We're not as primitive as you might expect, are we?"

Pam looked at the tall buildings whizzing by and the

eight lanes of traffic. "No, not at all. I love it here. All but the weather."

"I see by your articles that you've become quite a hockey expert."

"That's the most ironic thing of all! Every night I study books on the plays so that I can understand them. But I do enjoy it. It's so fast moving."

Wendy shuddered slightly. "It seems so rough-and-tumble to me. Violent, sort of. Those men seem so . . . wild."

Pam grinned to herself. Anyone who had a crush on Wendell Adams would have to think a hockey player was wild. Aloud she said, "By the way, Wendy, I did have dinner with Wendell Adams the other evening."

"Oh? How . . . nice." Hurt rang in Wendy's voice.

Pamela hurried to finish. "I think he'd like to know you better, Wendy. Would you come to dinner at my house some evening if he were there? Something casual, so you could visit?"

The pain fled from Wendy's eyes and a sparkle replaced it. "I'd like that, Pam. That is, if you wouldn't rather be alone with Wendell."

Being with Wendell was not unlike being all alone, Pam had decided after spending time with Tiger Evans. Wendell was definitely more Wendy's type.

"Not at all. We're just acquaintances. Let's plan to do it sometime over the Christmas holidays." Pam had been worrying about the holidays, squelching lonely thoughts when she could. Even one small party would help pass the evenings.

Before she could continue her thoughts, they arrived at the church and had to hurry inside. The Bible study was about to begin. Wendy's father was already speaking when they slipped into the back row.

"Today we will continue our study of Simon Peter. If you remember, last week we studied his capabilities as a leader of men. Some Biblical historians believe that Peter, as the active and vocal representative for the disciples, was responsible for many of the advances made during Jesus' ministry. To Peter, Jesus committed the task of rallying and leading the disciples after His departure."

Pam's mind drifted to another leader of men. Perversely, her mind kept comparing Ty to Simon Peter. Once she had begun to think of Peter as a human with weaknesses and foibles like her own, he became more real to her—and the miracles God wrought in him even more amazing.

Pastor Williamson was summarizing by the time Pam's attention traveled back to his words. "For all of Peter's faults and flaws, he still stands as a rich example of how a sympathetic, talented, dynamic, and spontaneous but imperfect man can be touched by love. Not only was Peter won over by God's love, he was enriched and deepened by training, disciplined by the hardships he faced, and ultimately used by God to be a bold and unforgettable instrument of His purpose."

Pam's sharp intake of breath caused Wendy to glance at her friend in concern. The wheels were spinning wildly in Pam's brain. Ty and the Biblical Peter were very much the same type of men! Perhaps there was hope for Ty after all. Where God worked, there were no limits.

Encouraged and uplifted, Pam chatted gaily with Wendy until her father joined them at the door.

"Well, Pamela, I'd like to congratulate you on your work," Reverend Williamson beamed.

"My work? I really haven't done much yet, Sir," Pam countered.

"Nonsense! You wrote a wonderful article on my favorite hockey player, Tiger Evans. I was delighted to see another side to the man. He's got the reputation for being a bit wild and rebellious. Your article shed a whole new light on him."

"Thank you." Pam bit her inner lip to keep a smile from spreading across her face.

"You, know, his name has always intrigued me," Wendy's father continued. "Tiger. Like a jungle cat. Dangerous. Sly. Handsome. In fact, that reminds me a bit of our Bible lesson today."

Pam's eyes flew open wide. From Ty to Simon Peter was a leap she had made during the course of the hour, but she couldn't imagine how the scholarly Reverend Williamson could make a connection.

Obviously seeing the question in the girl's eyes, he continued. "I'm talking about the names, of course. Tiger is a rather distinctive name, but it fits him. And Peter was a distinguishing name in his day as well. Simon was a rather common name in those days, but Peter was not. The name given to Simon, Peter or Cephas, soon superseded the name Simon. In part because it was a distinctive name and not commonly used. But perhaps Jesus' followers knew that the name carried significance not only for Peter the man but also for the life of the Church. I always think that those names hold special meaning and connote leaders. Strong men, Tiger and Peter, don't you agree? I wish that Tiger Evans were a professing Christian. What an example for young people he could be!"

Dumbfounded, Pam only nodded. Obviously Wendy's father saw the same potential for good in Ty that she did. But she already knew Ty's attitude about God and churches. He was as likely to show an interest as he was to never put on another pair of skates. The prospects were dim.

Pam spent the rest of the day curled into a ball on the couch writing long, newsy Christmas letters to her friends and family. It was difficult not to be in the Christmas spirit here, even if she had to spend it alone. Clean snow blanketed the ground nearly every morning, and colorful decorations abounded. It was like living in a Christmas card.

And this year she would have a real tree, not miniature lights strung across the huge ficus tree in her mother's living room. All the stores were open late, and Pam planned to spend the entire week exploring, attempting to discover just the right gift for everyone on her list.

But her plan was nearly thwarted at the outset by Ty Evans.

As Pam slipped the cover over her typewriter a voice from behind her inquired, "Any sports scoops in which I'd be interested?"

A shiver of recognition danced on her spine. Ty had come back.

She gathered her wits and coolly swung around in her chair.

"Hello, Ty. Nice to see you."

"It's nice to see you, too. You have ink on the tip of your nose."

Pam's hand flew to her face, and just as it began to dawn on her, Ty added, "Just teasing. Did you miss me?"

"Very funny. Why did you do that?"

"Just trying out a theory. It works in hockey and it works with you. Fake a shot and distract everyone, *then* put the puck in the net. Same theory. Just wanted to keep you off your guard. You're more fun."

"You're in a good mood tonight." Pam had to smile. He looked like an overgrown imp with sparkling golden eyes and an improbable red stocking cap on his head.

"It's almost Christmas. I like the music."

"Like 'Silent Night' and 'Oh, Come All Ye Faithful?' " Pam supplied.

"Nah. None of that churchy stuff. I like 'Santa Claus is Coming to Town.' "

He wouldn't be serious. Finally Pam stood and walked toward her coat locker. "Well, I take all this very seriously. If you'll excuse me, I have some shopping to do. I have to get my packages in the mail soon. I'm already behind schedule."

"You mean you can't come out and play?" Ty sounded like a disappointed five-year-old. The bruise on his cheek had faded to nothing more than a yellow tinge, and he looked wonderful.

"Play at what? I spend all day thinking and writing about sports. I need a change."

"How about going skating? I think you're ready for another lesson."

"No thanks. I think I'd rather go to the dentist for a root canal," Pam parried, not to be cajoled by this charming tempter.

"Then can I go shopping with you?" Ty had swept the stocking cap from his curls and held it tightly in both hands in front of him. The impish gleam had turned to puppy-dog pleading.

"Why are you so anxious to see me today, Ty? I've been around all week," Pam queried, a bit put out about his prior absence.

"I needed some time to think, Pam. About . . . things."

Brock Madsen, no doubt.

"How about if we go shopping together? I could buy some Christmas presents myself. What do you say?" Ty knew he had her now, and a grin was beginning to spread across his features.

"Oh, all right. Come on. You probably know better than I where to shop anyway."

"Right. And I know just the place for supper after the stores close. Do you have your car here?"

"No. I walked today. It hadn't been running quite right. Wendy's brother has been working on it, but I think it needs to be looked at again. Anyway, it's not very far to walk."

"So you're finally getting used to the cold."

"I'll never be *used* to it. But at least now I'm not afraid of being out in it."

"Well, I'm not sure that's so good either," Ty commented seriously. "You have to maintain a healthy respect for this weather. And if that car ever stalls on you, don't get out and walk."

"How else would I get help, Ty?" Pam chided. He was certainly turning serious suddenly.

"I'm not talking about in town, Pam. Out in the country. Stay with the car and wait for help. You've got a much better chance of survival if you just stay with the car. Put on your snow gear and stay put."

"Yessir. Now can we go shopping?"

Ty sighed and took her arm. "Come on, then. Just remember what I said if you ever get stuck in the country."

The streets were black and white ribbons of snow and ice. Steam and exhaust fumes clouded the air. Christmas shoppers swarmed on the downtown streets in packs. Pam felt a sudden surge of the Christmas spirit.

"What do you want to shop for first, Pam?" Ty asked, his head close to her ear. Pam could see an occasional passerby stare at them as they recognized her companion.

"Toys. I have several godchildren that I always remember at Christmas. They're the most fun to buy for."

"Toys it is then. Come on." Ty lead her through a cluster of people waiting for a bus and into a department store. Minutes later they were transported into a fairy land of toys stacked to the ceilings.

"I should certainly be able to find something in here!" Pam exclaimed. Dolls and stuffed animals beckoned from every corner.

"Me too." Ty's voice was muffled from behind a stack of teddy bears. Shortly he peered around a large koala with a stuffed grizzly perched on his shoulders. The bear's chin rested cozily on Ty's head.

"Don't get carried away, now. These aren't for grownups," Pam chided. Ty had discarded the bear for a kangaroo with a baby peeking from its pouch.

"Who says? I might do a little shopping myself in this department. You've given me an idea."

"What sort of idea?" Pam couldn't imagine a single idea that Ty hadn't already had—on any subject.

"Never mind. Just do your shopping." He smiled and disappeared behind a stack of dolls.

Pam scanned the shelves for sturdy, mailable items and amassed a small cluster on the counter. Before paying she decided to look for Ty. He was standing entranced before a display of baby dolls.

"What are you doing?" she inquired.

"Reading the boxes. Can you believe this?" Ty squinted at the fine print on the box of a golden haired infant.

"Believe what? What are you talking about?"

"I never had any sisters or paid much attention to dolls, but look at this—read all the things that these toys do. This one cries, this one crawls, this one roller skates," Ty pointed to each box as he enumerated their talents, "this one eats, this one burps, this one . . . ugh! Why would anyone want a doll to do that?"

By this time tears of laughter had come to Pamela's eyes. The laughter bubbled to the surface as a clerk came to inquire. "May I help you, Sir? Do you have any questions?"

"Yeh. Why would anyone want a doll that—"

"Ty!" Pam's staccato voice cut short his inquiry.

"Never mind," he murmured before adding, "I'll take one of each."

"One of each, Sir?" The clerk reiterated, unbelieving.

"Yeh. Except for that one," and he pointed. "That's disgusting. Nobody should have to buy diapers for a *doll*."

"What are you doing?" Pam tugged at his sleeve.

"Shopping. Are you done?"

"Almost. Why are you buying all those dolls?"

"To go with the trucks and stuffed animals." Ty

nodded to a growing stack of miniature vehicles and furry creatures.

"Do you have that many children in your family?" Pam gasped. He had amassed several hundred dollars worth of toys in their minutes in the store.

"No. There aren't any children in my family." The odd tone in his voice cut her short. She paid for her insignificant looking purchases as Ty pulled a wad of bills from his trouser pocket. When he was done counting out the money, only a few bills were left. Pam was still unused to the colorful Canadian money. "Play money," she always thought when she used it. But it bought what she wanted.

"Looks like dinner will be skimpy tonight." Ty waved the bills in front of her nose. "Unless, of course, I remembered my credit cards." He dug deeper in his pocket and pulled out a flat silver rectangle. "We're in luck! I can keep shopping and still afford a meal! Where do you want to go next?"

"Tiger Evans, what do you think you're doing? This is crazy. You've spent more than my entire paycheck on toys for children you don't have!"

"Is that all you get paid? Boy, I think I'll call your editor and have him give you a raise."

When he adamantly refused to respond to her inquiries, she finally gave up. Biting her tongue, she didn't even comment as he ordered the purchases delivered to his apartment. It was his business, after all, and though curiosity nearly consumed her, she remained quiet.

By nine o'clock Pam had finished most of her meager shopping, and Ty had purchased several pounds of imported chocolates and solid milk chocolate sculpture in the shape of a hockey stick. Lugging the parcels to the car, Pam began her questions again.

"Ty, why did you buy all these things? Toys? Chocolates?"

"Never mind. Just plan on coming with me tomorrow after work. I have practice until four. I'll pick you up at your apartment at five. Are you hungry?"

Still curious but resigned to wait, Pam nodded. She was about ready to dive into one of those boxes of chocolates.

"Starving."

"Good! I know just the place. A Japanese steak house."

It seemed a bit of a contradiction in terms to Pam, who envisioned all steak houses as salad bar, baked potato, and meat establishments, but Ty's choices hadn't disappointed her yet, and she nodded.

They were escorted into the dim recesses of a Japanese garden. A tiny river flowed under the bridge. As Pam's eyes became accustomed to the darkness she could see that there were no tables. Instead, chairs were clustered around individual grills, and a cook stood before each preparing food for their patrons.

Once settled, a tiny Oriental waitress came with menus and steaming washcloths on which to wipe their hands. Without glancing at the menus, Ty ordered, "Two Imperial dinners, please." Nodding briefly, the waitress slipped away.

"Imperial? Sounds too grand for me, Ty."

"Nothing is too grand for you, Miss Priss. Do you like lobster?" Ty slapped the washcloths around in his hands.

"Love it. But I never order it."

"How come?"

"The price of one lobster could feed a dozen starving children, Ty."

"Well, if a dozen starving children come in, I'll buy them each an Imperial dinner too. Loosen up, Pam. Enjoy."

Guiltily at first, then more unreservedly, she did. Course after course came and went, each more wonderful than the last. Fragrant, savory soup came with big china spoons. Than a delicate cucumber and crab salad. By the time Pam had finished her appetizer of chicken livers, mushrooms and onions cooked on the big grill before her, she was tugging at the waistband of her skirt.

"I'm getting full."

"Not yet, I hope. The best is yet to come." Ty had been visiting with the high-hatted cook as he theatrically tossed knives in the air, slicing and performing simultaneously. Pam's eyes grew rounder with each toss of the knife and each clatter of wooden salt and pepper grinders. She kept eating—mouthful after mouthful—until the final course.

"Ty, I can't eat another thing. Really."

"Just one spoonful. It's my favorite ice cream—mandarin chocolate. It's like orange sherbet with swirls of fudge in it. I guarantee that it's good!" He teased her lips with the tip of his spoon. As soon as she smiled, he slid the sample between her teeth.

"Oh!" Pam groaned and leaned back against the chair. "I won't ever eat again!"

"Not until tomorrow, at least," Ty added unsympathetically. He had a capacity for food Pamela couldn't fathom.

"You eat like a horse," she finally concluded.

He grinned and replied, "I also work out an average of six hours a day. And I've said it before, my appetites are voracious. All of them."

Suddenly uncomfortable with the tone of the conversation, Pam stood. "No comment, Mr. Evans. But I do need to get home. I have gifts to wrap."

Ty nodded evenly. "Then let's get going."

It had begun to snow again as they stepped into the street. Downy white flakes drifted from the sky. Pam turned her face upward to meet them.

"It tickles."

"I suppose it does. So do I, if you want to know."

She shot him a disparaging glance. "Don't you dare."

"You should know better than to tell me that." He grabbed her under the armpits and squeezed. Even through her coat, Pamela giggled. He had found her weakness. The two of them dodged and laughed in the snowy darkness until, breathless, Pam begged, "Take me home, Ty. I'll see you tomorrow."

"Awright." They piled into the low-slung car, showering snow over the leather seats. At Pam's apartment building Ty pulled into the visitor parking lot and jumped out to open her door.

"You don't have to see me in, Ty. I'm sure you must be tired," Pam assured him.

"Tired? Of what?" Ty seemed amused by the thought.

At a loss for an answer, Pam turned and walked through the double doors. She could sense more than hear Ty's catlike tread behind her. At her door, she turned to face him.

"Thank you for another lovely evening. Good night."

"Is that all? Good night?" Ty had insinuated his arm in front of her, blocking her from entering the apartment.

"I'm afraid it is." Pam's chin came up with a determined tilt. She had allowed herself to depend too much on this man. His absence the past few days had left her feeling empty and alone. For her own protection she needed to separate herself from him.

Without warning, Ty leaned over and caught the open lips with his own. Pam took a step backward, and her shoulder blades grazed the sleeve of his coat. Trapped. Tenderly. When he lifted his lips from her own, he smiled slightly, his thoughts hidden from her gaze.

"See you tomorrow, Prudish Pamela. Don't forget."

Forget? Ty had indelibly imprinted his memory on her lips. She knew deep inside her that whatever she did with the rest of her life, Tiger Evans would be a man she could never forget.

CHAPTER 6

"Hi! READY?" Ty's head came around the corner of the dividing bookcase that separated her desk from twelve others in the large office. The clatter of typewriters drowned the sudden rapid thudding in her chest. Tiger Evans could take her breath away. The tips of his golden curls were frozen and beads of ice lay on the shoulders of his creamy suede jacket.

"Cold outside?" Pam asked the obvious question, stalling for time while her equilibrium returned to normal.

"No, Prudish Pamela. My hair always freezes to my head." Ty rumpled the brittle curls. "Of course it's cold outside. What do you think?"

"Then why on earth didn't you dry your hair before coming here?"

"Practice went on longer than usual. By the time I got showered it was time to leave. Aren't you glad to see me?" He lifted both eyebrows and slid one slim hip onto her paper-filled desk.

"Of course I am. But I don't relish the idea of nursing you back to health after a bout of pneumonia. I think you'd be a terrible patient."

"I'm rather charming when I'm sick in bed. You know, vulnerable, appealing, sweet."

He was displaying those very attributes as they spoke, Pam concluded. He could be as soft and amiable off the ice as he was tough and unyielding on it. The more she saw of Ty Evans the more complex he became.

"Well, if you want to land in the hospital, that's your choice, but I don't want to be a part of it." Pam shuffled the papers before her.

"Are you sure? That's my next stop—the hospital."

Pam shot him a worried look, but his robust appearance allayed any fears for his own health. "Hospital? Do you have someone to visit there?"

A bleakness flickered momentarily and was replaced with a bright twinkle. "Are you coming with me to find out?"

Sighing, Pam nodded. "And if they have a psychiatric ward, let's stop and get your head checked. I think your brain has frostbite."

"I promise to never pick you up with a wet head again. But if I'm late, you have to promise not to nag."

A warm glow licked its way upward in Pam's torso. Each time Ty referred to a "next time" she clutched at the words with hope. He had become so important that the thought of never having a "next time" was beginning to frighten her.

His car was running at the building's entrance.

"Ty, how do you dare leave the car running?" Pam gasped.

"I carry two keys and just lock it. Here, get in. It should be nice and warm." He opened the door, and she slipped into the cozy interior. Once again, the smells of fresh soap and lime assaulted her nostrils. She leaned back against the head rest and closed her eyes.

"Well, here we are."

Pam's eyes flew open. The car was parked in a large, bleak lot facing a hospital.

"Ty? You weren't kidding?" she squeaked.

"No. Didn't you believe me?" He slipped out of the car and held her door. "Let's go inside instead of staring at the architecture."

Pam stumbled a bit as she followed him. This seemed an unlikely place to visit for fun.

Inside the door two young nurses were waiting.

"Hello, Mr. Evans! How are you?"

"Fine, thanks. Did you get those boxes I sent?"

"Yes. They're up on third floor. Do you need any help?" Two pair of round eyes pleaded to be of assistance, but Ty declined.

"No, thanks. I'll take care of it myself. Come on, Pam."

Bewildered, Pam trudged along beside him, her snow boots making a crisp, grating sound against the highly polished tile.

"Ugh! I hate the smell of hospitals!" Ty exclaimed as they neared the elevator. On Pam's empty stomach the vapors made her feel nauseous. She hoped Ty's mission was a brief one.

She forgot her affliction as they stepped from the elevator and onto the children's ward. Tiny faces peered at them expectantly. A buxom head nurse accosted them as they neared the desk.

"Mr. Evans! We've been waiting for you! The children are sick with curiosity."

"Well, if that's the worst thing that any of them are suffering, we're in good shape," Ty commented dryly. But he smiled, and the big woman returned the smile. She and Ty seemed to be partners in a conspiracy that Pam knew nothing about.

"Hi! Tiger! Made any points lately?" A little voice came from the back of the ward.

"What do you think, kid?" Ty tousled a few small heads as he walked toward the voice.

"I think you can't miss. That's what my dad says."

"You tell your dad he's a smart man." Ty stopped before the end of the bed and looked at a wan little fellow whose coloring matched the white of the sheets.

Pam followed Ty hesitantly. These children were expecting him, it was obvious. Even the children from the private rooms were on the ward in wheelchairs. Only she seemed unaware of what he was here for.

"The nurses said you had something for us, Tiger. What is it?" A pale boy with a robust voice inquired.

"Hang on, buddy. I'd like you to meet a friend of mine first. This is Pamela Warren." Ty took the bewildered Pam by the elbow and spun her around for the children to see. "And you really have Pam to thank for our being here, because she's the one who gave me the idea to come here today."

"What are you talking about?" Pam hissed through a smile. That knock on the head had finally done its damage to Ty's brain.

"You see," Ty continued, obviously aware that the children were hanging on every word, "Pam was buying presents for Christmas. We were in the toy department, and she was picking out things to send to Arizona for the children she knew. Well," and Ty paused theatrically for effect, "I don't know many children, so I had nothing to do. So that's when I decided that I'd do some Christmas shopping too and then find some children who might like a present. Do you guys know of any?"

The din that the question set up didn't subside for some moments. By the time the room had quieted, Ty was passing out boxed gifts wrapped in red and green foil. As he passed Pamela, he whispered in her ear, "The red boxes with gold bows are for girls. The green with silver are for boys. Help me out."

Tears pricked at the back of Pam's eyes as she watched the children tear into the elaborately wrapped gifts and pull toys from the boxes. The stuffed grizzly bear was there, and the kangaroo. One tiny girl's eyes widened at the sight of a roller-skating doll while another lovingly rocked a pink-cheeked baby doll in her arms.

Ty was on the floor in the middle of the ward assembling a farm set, and three little boys leaned across his shoulders and head peering at the miraculous set-up. The smallest had his fingers wound tightly in Ty's curls.

"Hey! Mr. Tiger! There's still another box of presents!" Out from behind the door came two small boys pulling yet another cache of packages.

"But everyone here has one; don't they?" Ty asked innocently.

The children glanced around the room, obviously disappointed that there was no one left to whom to give the gaily wrapped gifts.

"The nurses don't have any!" The wan boy in the big bed piped. Ty grinned at him and pointed a finger his way. "Good thought, big fellow. Do you think we should do anything about it?"

"Give them the presents!"

"Yeh! Are they full of toys too?"

"Have the nurses open them!"

The children's voices chimed together. Laughing, Ty stretched a hand toward the box. "The children obviously want you to have these. You'd better open them." Inside were all the chocolates Pam had drooled over, and the delighted nurses began sampling the savory fare.

There was one large foil-covered box left. Ty picked up it and tucked it under his arm. With a sweep of his head he indicated that Pam should follow him. They slipped from the noisy ward unnoticed and started for the elevator. Pam was quiet for some moments as they sped upward, too touched to speak.

"Ty, that was simply beautiful" she finally managed.

102

He smiled slightly and said, "It was more fun for me than for them, Pam. A purely selfish act."

Overwhelmed by his modesty, Pam clamped her teeth over her lower lip. He was even more of a hero than she had given him credit for.

"Here we are. Do you want to come in?" Ty pulled her off the elevator and into the corridor.

"Where are we?" Pam glanced around. This was a far more serious looking floor than pediatrics. Heart monitors and other unidentifiable but intimidating looking machines lined the halls.

"Brock Madsen's room. I haven't seen him since the accident. Guess I've been putting it off, but now's the time." There was an unfamiliar tension in Ty's visage, and he looked slightly sick. Doing this apparently gave him a more severe case of nerves than any opponent on ice.

"I'll come if you want me to. Maybe you'd rather be alone."

"Come. I'm not sure I can think of a lot of small talk with a guy who might lose his eyesight. Your presence might help."

Pam felt a gut-wrenching churning in her stomach. No wonder Ty had put this off. Even she felt the urge to turn heel and run. But the slump of Ty's shoulders made her realize that—for once—he needed her to be strong. Facing the embodiment of one's most private fears was not for the faint-hearted. That Ty chose to do it in her presence was a gratifying—and humbling—event.

"Let's go then. Do you know what the doctors have to say?"

"He's had some surgery. I think he's still in bandages, and I know he has to be quiet. Some of the other guys have been up to see him, but no one seems to want to talk about it. It could have been any one of us. . . ."

Through the half-open door Pam could see a dark-haired man lying flat on a hospital bed, his head swathed in bandages. Instinctively she knew that it was Brock Madsen. Ty moved ahead of her into the room.

"You'll do just about anything to lay around in bed and not have to practice, won't you Madsen?" he groaned softly, taking the prone man by the hand.

A smile lit the other man's features. "Is that you, Ty? I've been waiting for you to come and see me." He clutched the fingers Ty offered like a lifeline.

"Yeh? Well, I've been waiting for you to come to me. I guess you won this round, but don't expect me to weaken so easily again. I even brought you a present."

"Is it a girl?" Brock was obviously struggling for whatever normalcy he could muster.

"Well, I brought a girl, but you can't have her. I found her in the parking lot after a game one night. You can go and look for your own. Come here, Pam. Brock, I want you to meet my friend, Pam Warren."

Pam edged near the bed. Ty's voice was so casual and normal that she was stunned by the look in his eyes. Anguish welled there when he glanced at his friend. She put her hand across Madsen's limp one and gave a tiny squeeze.

"Nice to meet you, Mr. Madsen. Ty's talked about you."

"Nothing bad, I hope?"

"Terrible things, actually, but I don't believe him," Pam teased, sensing the need for lightness.

"She's got your number, Tiger. Good for her. You need someone who can outfox you."

Ty snorted in disdain, "Madsen, you couldn't outfox a paper bag and neither could she. Do you want to find out what I brought you or not?"

"So hand it over." Madsen stretched his hands out before him. Ty winced at the sight of the empty, searching hands midair and tugged the wrapping paper

104

from the box. Nestled in a brown, pleated paper cup was the large chocolate hockey stick. Ty took it from the box and laid it in Brock's hands. Brock fingered the shape and his hands fell around it with instinctive familiarity. Finally, he commented, "A little short, isn't it? How high is the goalie?"

Ty chuckled. "Now lick your fingers."

Brock lifted a tentative finger to his lips, and as the tart sweetness hit his tastebuds he smiled. "Awright! Something to eat besides gelatin, ground beef, and green beans!"

"You never ate any better than that when you cooked at home." Ty commented.

"And you cooked even less, so don't criticize my culinary habits, Evans. You did good to bring me this—don't go and blow it now."

Pam watched the two friends interact. All the rough, playful banter only proved their fondness for each other, and one more facet of Ty's multi-sided character was sparkling in new light.

It was nearly seven o'clock when Ty finally said, "Well, buddy. Gotta go. I've got a girl here who needs supper."

"She can stay and eat with me," Brock offered.

"You'd want her for dessert. Sorry. No deal. Take it easy and let me know if you need anything." Ty touched the hand lying on the bed.

"Okay. Thanks." Madsen's words were so soft Pam could hardly hear them as they slipped from the room. Pulling the door closed behind him, Ty leaned heavily against the wall and sighed a deep, almost tearful sigh.

"Ty?" she ventured hesitantly. He sagged against the concrete wall, depleted.

"I'm okay, Pam. It was just more difficult than I'd anticipated, that's all."

Pam grasped the limp hand hanging at his side and pulled him toward the elevator. "Let's go now. I know Brock appreciated your visit. He seemed almost hungry for company."

Ty snorted derisively. "That's because none of his friends want to see him this way, Pam. We're a big tough bunch until we have to come face to face with the fact that it could be one of us lying there."

"Ty," Pam ventured, daring for the first time to express a fear of her own, "have you ever thought of giving up hockey? You've got so much education—you don't need to play hockey for a living. Have you ever wanted to get into something—"

"Safer? No. Hockey isn't any worse than other professional sports. We might tend to brawl a little more but otherwise it's safe. The accidents are freaky things, like Brock's injury. Just an unlucky coincidence."

Freaky things . . . unlucky coincidence. Michael had said the very same things to her—three days before he died in a fiery crash. Suddenly the parallel seemed startlingly clear. A knot of fear sprang deep within her. She couldn't bear to lose another friend as she'd lost Michael. A part of her had died with him. To lose Ty as well would be her undoing.

"Cheer up, Pamela. You look like you just lost your best friend!" Outside the hospital Ty's demeanor changed, and he was much like his old self, joking playfully.

But the seeds of fear had been planted and grew in Pam's fertile imagination. Quelling her dark thoughts, Pam gave Ty a quavery smile. "Sorry. I guess seeing your friend had an effect on me as well."

"Brock would be furious if he thought he'd depressed my date. He's a real ladies' man, you know. For his sake, I think we should go out and have some fun. What do you say?"

"That reminds me, Ty! Would you like to come to my house for dinner one evening soon? I'd like to have Wendell—"

"Wendell? What do you want me there for? To chaperon?" Ty's voice was disgruntled.

"No, Silly! I'm inviting Wendell so he can get to know my friend Wendy better. I thought if you came we'd have a foursome. Could you?"

"Ah! Wendell is for Wendy! That sounds much better. I thought maybe this Wendell creep was horning in on my territory," Ty joked, but Pam hoped for a serious tone in his voice. Being considered Tiger Evans' "territory" was flattering indeed.

"Could you?" she persisted.

"I suppose. If I'm here."

"Where will you be going?" Pam asked, surprised.

"I'm a hockey player, remember? We take road trips. The teams don't always come to us. I was on one a few days ago. Have you forgotten?"

Relief and embarrassment flooded through Pam. She was still reminded what a novice she was to sports reporting. It had not occurred to her that he would go on a road trip. There was so much to learn!

Ty was asking a question as her mind snapped back to the present. "So what night is that big event?"

"Well, Ty, it's hardly that big an event! Just a dinner for friends."

"Playing cupid is always a big event, Pam." Ty grinned impishly. "Just don't shoot yourself in the foot with one of Cupid's arrows."

"Very funny. How about tomorrow night? Will you be here then?"

Ty nodded. "This weekend we have our last away games before Christmas. What time do you want me there?"

"I'll say seven. If it doesn't work out for Wendy or Wendell, I'll call you."

"Good enough. Now, where do you want to eat?" They were cruising aimlessly down a stretch of road.

"Oh! I won't have time to eat, Ty. Just drop me off at home. I have grocery shopping to do if I'm going to be ready for tomorrow night."

"You have to eat. I'll take you to the grocery store, and then we'll go get a sandwich. You'd better enjoy it now. I'll be gone all weekend."

Pam felt a gnawing emptiness in her stomach at the thought. She had come to depend on Ty for a great deal. She dreaded his absence. "When you put it that way, how can I resist?"

Ty only smiled and pulled into a parking lot.

Shopping with Tiger Evans was a little like running an obstacle course. Fans tended to cluster at the end of the aisle in which they were shopping, and Ty stopped several times to autograph scraps of paper and even the side of a large box of disposable diapers. As he talked to the crowd, Pam hastily threw groceries into her cart. Steaks. Wild rice. Mushrooms. Cherry tomatoes. Lettuce. Baby carrots. Whipping cream.

"Are you done yet?" Ty wandered up behind her.

"Almost. Is there anything special that you'd like for dessert?" Pam was studying the pastry counter.

"There certainly is."

Pam felt Ty's hands slip around her inside her coat, and his fingers began to knead softly the hollows under her rib cage. She froze, acutely aware of his meaning.

She turned toward him and his hands remained under her coat, now caressing the small of her back. "Sorry, Ty. That's not on the menu."

"But you're the most delicious thing in the store, Pam. And I don't want anything else."

"Then I'll only buy cream puffs for three." Pam pulled away from his intimate grasp.

"All right, Prudish Pamela. You do that. But remember, I won't be satisfied until I get the dessert I want."

They were both quiet as they returned to Pam's after a quick supper. Ty carried her groceries to the door and put them on the floor. He ran his hands

108

across the shoulders of her coat and studied her with an inquiring gaze.

Reading the question in his eyes, Pam answered. "I don't think you should come in tonight, Ty. I have lots to do. See you tomorrow at seven?" The bright tone in her voice belied her nervousness. Ty seemed determined to force this relationship a step further. And he wanted things she couldn't give.

He turned to leave and then, spinning about, came back to stand in front of her. "Think about this, Pamela. I don't like being kept at arm's length. This could be a nice relationship—for both of us." He drew a single finger along the line of her cheek. Then dropping his hand to his side he turned and walked away, leaving Pam gaping at her front door.

She was trembling slightly as she stepped into her apartment. The intimacy Ty wanted she couldn't give without the bonds of marriage. But Tiger Evans was as free as the jungle cat for which he was nicknamed. Was she woman enough to tame him?

Pam was becoming nervous waiting for her guests to arrive. It was her very first dinner party and she wanted it to be perfect. Wendy had been blatantly excited over the prospect of having Wendell Adams as a dinner partner, but she'd expressed less delight at the thought of Ty Evans's presence.

"Oh, Pam! Ty Evans! The hockey player? He's rather famous! I don't think he'd enjoy having dinner with *me!*"

"Don't be silly, Wendy. Ty is very nice and easy to talk to. You'll like him."

"I don't know . . . he seems so—intimidating—to me. He's so large and rough. I've watched him skate on television. I don't know what I'd say to him!"

"Then let him begin the conversation. Just relax. Do you want to have dinner with Wendell or not?" Pam was becoming irritated by her friend's hesitance.

"Of course I do!"

"Then Tiger is part of the package. See you at seven."

Pam was beginning to fear that Wendy had chickened out just as the doorbell rang. Giving a big sigh of relief she ran to answer it.

"Am I late?" Wendy came bursting into the room shaking snow from her shoulders.

"No. In fact, you're the first one here. I was beginning to think I'd been stood up." Pam took the snowy coat and hung it in the closet. Then she turned to study her friend. Wendy had worked very hard on her appearance. Pam could see the unfamiliar pencilings of make-up around her eyes and a more than natural rosy glow on her cheeks. Even the dress was new.

"You look great, Wendy. Wendell should be impressed."

"Humph! He'll never even notice me when he sees you! You're so beautiful, Pam. And it comes so naturally! I could never get by in an outfit like that, and it looks like a dream on you!"

Pam spread her fingers across the soft suede jumpsuit she was wearing. There were no hems in the garment and the leather fell in ragged edges at her wrists and ankles. She wore thonglike suede sandals on her feet and no make-up at all on her face. Her golden curls cascaded across her shoulders, and her dark eyes gleamed warm and bright.

"Thanks, Wendy. I've always loved this outfit but there aren't many places appropriate for it. I guess it's meant for lounging around or quiet dinner parties at home. I hope Ty likes it."

"He'd have to be blind not to."

A dart of pain shot through Pamela. Blind. Ty had called this morning to tell her that Brock Madsen's prognosis was becoming grimmer and grimmer. With each negative report, Pam feared more and more for Ty's own well-being. Before she could continue with her negative meditation, the doorbell rang again.

Wendell stood at the door, muffler concealing all but his frosty glasses.

"Come on in, Wendell. Take off your coat. You know my friend Wendy, don't you?" Pam kept up an idle patter as the two eyed each other, sizing up the situation. Just as she got the pair ensconced on the couch, the bell rang again.

"Hi, Miss Priss. Is the food ready?" Ty bolted into the room shaking snow from his shoulders like a big wet golden retriever. He made up for her other guests' timidity and planted a noisy kiss on the hostess's lips. From under his coat he pulled a florist's bundle. Wendy and Wendell stared at him as though a craft from outer space had just landed.

"Roses! Thank you, Ty!" Pam buried her nose in the fragrant buds forgetting for a moment her other guests.

"And who have we here?" Ty was studying the pair frozen into immobility on the couch.

He *was* intimidating, Pam decided. He was wearing tight-fitting trousers that delineated every line of muscle and sinew in his legs. He also wore a trim-fitting linen shirt and an unconstructed suit jacket. The top buttons of his shirt were undone and his knit tie was knotted loosely mid-chest. He'd jammed his hands in his pockets to study the other guests. He looked like a very large athlete that had stepped from the pages of *Gentleman's Quarterly*. His blond curls rioted across his forehead.

"Ty, I'd like you to meet Wendy Williamson and Wendell Adams."

"Pleased to meet you." Ty grinned impishly at the pair on the couch, amused by their discomfort. He began to prowl the room restlessly. His movements seemed only to make Wendy and Wendell more nervous.

"Food's ready. Let's eat!" Pam called from the kitchen. She knew that Wendell and Wendy would stay frozen on the couch unless she pried them loose. She had forgotten how awesome Ty's presence could be to the uninitiated.

Once they were seated, Pam looked to Wendell. "Would you say grace?" She bowed her head, but the feeling never left her that Ty was studying her thoughtfully. After the prayer she glanced at Ty. His head remained unbowed, but he had a quizzical look in his eye.

Ignoring the unasked questions, Pam guided her guests through the meal. By dessert—which happened to include a cream puff for Ty—even Wendy and Wendell were beginning to enjoy themselves. Ty could be witty and charming if he desired, and he poured it all forth on the shy couple.

After dinner they were all seated in Pam's tiny living room. For once Pam was glad for the congestion as she found herself nestled under Ty's arm on the couch.

"Did you know that there's a string quartet at the Convention Centre tonight? Somebody famous, I think," Ty commented. Pam glanced at him in surprise. What did he care about a string quartet?

"Yes. It sounded wonderful. But the tickets were rather expensive." Wendy sighed.

"I'd looked at the announcements too," chimed Wendell, "but the price was really out of reach."

"You mean you'd go if you had tickets?" Ty queried, squeezing Pam as he spoke.

"Oh, yes!" the pair chimed together.

"Well, I've got tickets if you want them." Ty used his free arm to pull an envelope from his shirt pocket. "Here. Take them."

"Oh, no! They're much too expensive. And we're Pam's guests!" Wendy cried, looking longingly at the envelope.

"Nonsense. I have a season ticket, and I rarely attend. I'm usually on the road or just forget about it.

Take them. I can stay here and entertain Pam. Right, Pamela?''

Pam shot him a grin before adding, "Please go, you two. I know you'd enjoy it. But you'd better hurry. You only have about fifteen minutes.''

The two were out the door and down the hall when Ty whispered in Pam's ear, "Did you notice that they were holding hands when they left?''

Her answer was an elbow in his midsection. "You crafty animal! You had that planned!''

"It worked, didn't it? I thought you said you wanted them to get together. Now they are.''

"And what about the tickets?'' Pam put her hands to her hips.

"Truth! I do have a season ticket. My parents buy it for me every year for Christmas. And I never go to a concert. It's like everything else my parents have ever done for me—it has no relationship to what I enjoy. I'm glad someone can use them. Now, how would you like me to keep you company?''

Ty slid his arms around her waist and swung her around. She felt light as air in his embrace. Shortly she found herself on the couch again as Ty shrugged out of his jacket. When he sat down she curled into his outstretched arm.

They sat quietly for a few moments. Then Pam asked the question that had been burning in her mind. "Ty?''

"Hum?'' He stretched lazily beside her.

"What about your parents?''

She felt him stiffen, but his voice was still casual as he answered, "What about them?''

"You rarely talk about them. And when you do it's with such scorn. If I didn't know you better, I'd think you hated them.''

"Then you don't know me very well at all, Pam, because I *do* hate them.''

Pamela gasped unconsciously at the malice in his tone. "No! I can't believe that!''

"Fine. Then don't believe it. And don't bring up my family again."

"Ty—"

"Don't get into it, Pam. You won't like it." His golden eyes were dark, the liquid pools brimming with pain. A nervous twitch ran along Ty's jaw line, and he clenched and unclenched his fists.

An uncomfortable, nearly palpable silence fell between them. Pam was at a loss for words, and Ty seemed unwilling to talk. Finally he ventured in a strange, hoarse tone, "You must have had a happy childhood, Pamela."

She nodded thoughtfully. "Yes. I suppose I did. My parents were terribly overprotective though. Sometimes I felt like a sheltered flower. I was like a caged bird, dreaming of flying free."

"And that's why you came up here?"

Nodding, Pam continued, "All that loving concern was becoming stifling. My father ruled my life with an iron hand. He chose my friends and even my clothes. I know it was because of love that he acted as he did, but I needed to get away. I was stretching my wings, and it made him nervous. I thought it was better to do it far away where he couldn't try to control that too."

"But you love him?" Ty asked. Pam raised her eyebrow at the odd question.

"Of course. And he loves me. His flaws and mistakes are the result of that love. He kept me innocent of life far too long. It's good that you understand that, Ty. I know you think I'm funny and prim and proper—a really 'goodie two-shoes,' but I've never lived away from my family before, and I can't be rushed."

"Did your father approve of this outfit?" Ty asked, running his finger across the creamy softness of the leather.

"No," Pam laughed. "He nearly went through the ceiling. He wanted me to remain in the blazers and pleated skirts I wore as a schoolgirl. He told me it made me look too 'old.' I think it was a shock to him when I reminded him that I was twenty-two. But he raised me well, Ty. He gave me a fine education and a firm foundation of faith in God. My father is far from perfect, but he's very dear to me."

"You're a rather forgiving sort."

"I didn't have much to forgive, Ty. Do you?" Pam regretted the words as she spoke them. Ty's face convulsed in pain, and he spat out an oath at which Pam could only guess the meaning. He jumped to his feet and began prowling the room.

"I know you think I'm being an ungrateful son, Pam, but I can't love my father—or forgive him. He's done too many unforgivable things to me." Ty paused and studied the alarmed girl on the couch. "But maybe you'd like to see for yourself. We have our annual visit this time of year. I go for my mother's sake. She still thinks Christmas is a time for families. She should have learned after all these years that it never works out."

Pam drew in a sharp breath. Could she believe her ears? Ty Evans was offering to take her to meet his family—the family kept so much in the background of his much-publicized life.

"That's your decision, Ty. Not mine. But I'm glad you go—for your mother's sake. I'm sure it means a great deal to her."

"It doesn't mean a thing, Pam. She just needs to be able to tell her friends that her son was over during the Christmas holidays. What good is giving birth to a local celebrity if you can't brag about it? Mother is weak, Pam. Weak and easily controlled. If she'd cared anything for me she never would have stayed in the same house as my father. But status and money were far more important than any child's happiness. Maybe you'll begin to understand if you meet them."

Pam's head was spinning with the turn the conversation had taken. The bitter hatred in Ty's voice was terrifying but not so much as the stark, wounded look in his eyes. Whatever had transpired between father and son had taken a devastating toll.

"Are you sure you want to take me? It might ruin your reputation as a man of mystery."

Ty laughed. "Anything I tell you is 'off the record,' isn't it? Maybe it's time I shared my family with someone else, although I doubt you could ever understand them."

"But they're local business people, Ty. It's not as if you have them tucked away in a mountain retreat somewhere!"

"My father doesn't make intimate friends, Pam. I'd wager there aren't two people other than my mother and myself who know what he's really like. Perhaps you'll have to see for yourself what I mean."

"When, Ty?"

"Sunday. I'll be back from the road trip and it's the day before Christmas Eve. That's close enough to December 25th to allow my mother to say I was home for Christmas—and it gives me all day on the 24th to get the bad taste out of my mouth."

Pam nodded dumbly. "What should I wear?" She realized as soon as she spoke what a shallow question it was, but Ty smiled slightly.

"You could wear the crown jewels and it wouldn't impress my father, so dress to please me, Pam. Help me get through the day." He grabbed her hand and kneaded the knuckles gently.

A shiver of trepidation bolted through her and brought with it a startling realization. Ty Evans was frightened—of his own father.

CHAPTER 7

IT HAD TAKEN PAMELA THE HOURS between church and 4:00 PM to prepare for her visit to the Evans' household. She had tried on every garment in her closet and discarded it on the bed before she settled on her first choice. The pale blue dress draped softly at the neckline framing her face. Her hair gleamed from laborious grooming and the finely applied make-up made her seem artifice-free. Even she had picked up some of Ty's nervousness about the afternoon.

Ready and waiting for Ty to arrive, Pam sank onto her couch and folded her hands to pray. Whatever demons kept Ty and his father estranged were bigger than she could manage alone. Turning everything over to God, she finally felt a sense of peace about the situation. All she could do for Ty was pray for him and give him her support—whether he wanted it or not.

The doorbell rang. Jumping to her feet to answer it, Pam smoothed the soft fabric of her dress across her legs. If she couldn't please his father, at least perhaps she could please Ty.

"Hi, Pam. Ready to go?" Ty stood in the doorway like a giant creature of some frozen region. He wore a different fur coat than the one Pam had seen him in previously. It hung open revealing a proper navy suit and white shirt brightened only by the slash of a red necktie.

"Sure. You look wonderful, Ty! I've never seen you so dressed up."

He smiled briefly, a hollow, empty smile that never reached his eyes. "Once a year I do this—so enjoy. My mother has the suits tailor-made in Hong Kong, and Dad orders a coat made up in his workroom. This is this year's Christmas offerings." He pulled the coat open by the pockets. Pam could see his initials monogrammed into the lining.

"Fur coats, custom suits, concert tickets—whatever the problem with your parents is, it can't be a lack of generosity," Pam commented.

Ty gave her a pitying smile. "That's exactly the problem with them, Pam. They can give most anything that money can buy—but that's not what really counts."

More and more bewildered by his attitude, Pam fell silent and shrugged into her simple cloth coat. She felt almost peasantlike next to Ty's magnificent fur. She had finally become accustomed to men wearing furs when she had come to this climate. It only seemed to make sense where many days the temperature rising to freezing was considered a "heat wave."

"In what part of the city do your parents live?" Pam watched the streets speed by.

"They live on the river. It's an old home but still considered elite. They'd move if they thought people regarded it otherwise." Ty's voice had taken on a sharp, warning note.

Pam fell silent until they pulled in front of a massive structure, and he stopped the car. "This is your parent's home?" she gasped, taking in the sloping dormers, arched doorways, and bay windows.

118

"Something simple for simple folk," Ty commented sarcastically. "My father always wanted a house with a parapet, and Mother likes lots of fireplaces. Well, this joint has it all except a resident ghost. I guess you don't need that when you have as many skeletons in the closets as my family does. Well, what are we waiting for? Come on inside."

A leaden weight slowed Pam's footsteps. The imposing house finally made her realize how totally out of her element she was. Ty Evans was not only famous, but wealthy. Perhaps his troubles were also more than she had imagined. Her simple lifestyle had not prepared her for any of this.

Then the front door swung open and whatever notions Pamela had of fleeing were dashed.

"Tyler, darling! Merry Christmas!" A slim woman in a black sheath stood in the doorway. Pamela's first impression was that of a diamond-encrusted ferret. The cloying scent of musk enveloped her like a cloud.

"Hello, Mother." Ty took a hesitant step forward. Pam could sense the stiffness in his usually agile gait. He leaned forward to allow the older woman to kiss him possessively on the cheek and straightened up quickly As he turned toward Pam she could see disgust and revulsion in his eyes.

"Ty . . ." Pam grabbed for his sleeve, frightened by the abhorrence she saw there, but as she did a shuttered look came over him, and she could no longer read his emotions.

"Mother, can we come in or shall we stand on the step all evening?"

"Please come in! I'm just so happy to have you here that I've forgotten my manners. Come in! And introduce me to your friend!"

As Pam's startled gaze adjusted as the ferrety face softened to that of a thin woman of fifty-odd years and nervous, darting eyes. *She's as nervous as Ty!* The thought surprised Pam, and she wondered even more about this odd, warring family.

119

"This is Pamela Warren, Mother. She's recently moved to Manitoba from the States. Arizona, to be exact. Pam, this is my mother, Marie Evans."

"Hello, Mrs. Evans. I'm pleased to meet you." Pam extended a hand toward Ty's mother, acutely aware of the inexpensive winter coat she wore.

But Pam's self-consciousness soon changed to compassion as she felt the tremble in the older woman's grip. Whatever nervousness she felt as a visitor was multiplied thrice over in her hostess.

Ty seemed unwilling to put either of them at ease, and he stood uncomfortably in the vast foyer shifting his weight from foot to foot delaying whatever came next.

"Let me hang up your coats. Where are my manners?" Marie helped Pam slide from her garment as Ty tugged the heavy beaver coat from his shoulders. "Go into the living room. Your father is just reading the paper. The poor man gets so tired these days before Christmas. Every beau and husband seems to want to buy his lady a fur this year. You know, don't you, Ty, how hard your father works?" There was an odd pleading in Marie's tone. It was as though she were saying, "Be nice, Ty, try to understand."

"Poor Father." Ty reiterated the words in an odd unsympathetic inflection, but he led the way into the massive living room of the Evans' home.

Pam's peripheral vision caught sight of large oil portraits of Evans' ancestors staring down at them with cold, impassive gazes. Ornate side tables holding vases of cut flowers rested beneath each baroque-framed canvas. Stiff-backed chairs with clawlike feet and armrests marched around the room, daring anyone to attempt to sit in them. Mr. Evans held court in the most comfortable part of the room where two soft, modern-day easy chairs were grouped in front of a roaring fire. He looked up as the two approached him.

"Hello, Tyler."

"Father."

Dumbstruck, Pam watched the barely cordial exchange between father and son who hadn't seen each other for nearly a year. Tyler got his golden handsomeness from the older man, it was obvious. Mr. Evans had a lionlike head of bright hair, worn longer than his son's and kept in check with volumes of hair cream. While Ty's catlike eyes always seemed warm and pleasant, his father's were cold and predatory. Already they were sizing her up.

"And who is the girl?"

"The 'girl,' as you so charmingly put it, is Pamela Warren. She's recently moved here from Arizona." Ty was already struggling to hold his temper in check.

"Miss Warren, pleased to meet you." Finally the older man stood, and Pam drew a shallow breath. He was taller than Ty, but thinner. He had none of the solid athletic muscles with which his son had been blessed, but he seemed powerful nonetheless. Even Ty seemed to cringe beneath his gaze.

Then Marie Evans bustled into the room. "Cook says we can eat immediately. So come, all of you, into the dining room. You can continue your little visit there."

Pam thought wildly that the "little visit" was about over if these two men didn't adjust their attitudes to one another quickly. She shot Ty a pleading glance. He looked at her for a long moment and then winked. Silently, he mouthed the words, "Okay, I'll try," and ushered her toward the waiting table.

Pam's breath caught in her throat as she spied the dazzling display. The room fairly shimmered with crystal and candles. Each place setting had more pieces of silverware than for which she could imagine uses. Crystal salt cellars and tiny individual flower vases sat at each place.

"What a lovely table!" she gasped.

Marie Evans smiled, pleased. "Thank you, dear. I always try to make it special when Tyler comes. Look, Tyler—I'm using the new goblets you sent me for Christmas. You made a lovely choice. Please, sit down."

Ty helped Pam into her seat, and his father escorted his mother to her chair. It was like an etiquette demonstration being played out before her. Shortly a maid in black with a white ruffled pinafore and frilly hat carried a seafood cocktail from the kitchen. Ty picked up the proper short-tined fork and nudged her in the arm.

"Follow me; I'll lead you through this sea of silver," he whispered.

Pam caught the disapproving look Mr. Evans's shot Ty's way. In this household Ty Evans was still a naughty little boy.

The family began to eat without a blessing, and Pam unobtrusively bowed her head to give thanks and plead for strength to get through this odd, tension-packed evening. She caught Ty's eye as she raised her head and could see an approving gleam there. Apparently being brave enough to flaunt custom was admirable to him.

The luscious food kept sticking in her throat as the meal progressed. Ty was silent, his father taciturn, and his mother struggling bravely to keep a modicum of civility in the meal.

"Tell me, Pamela. Where did you meet Tyler?"

"I interviewed him for the paper, actually. On my first day here. And, being a stranger to cold weather, he took pity on me and helped me with my car which was too cold to start."

"Finally learned some manners, then." Mr. Evans' voice startled them all. Three pairs of surprised eyes turned his way.

"Edward. . . ." Pam cold hear a warning in Mrs. Evans' voice, but her husband ignored the caution.

"We waited eighteen years, and he hadn't learned any by them. It's nice to hear he has finally come round after all." Edward Evans commented calmly as though he were discussing the weather instead of his grown son's supposed misbehavior.

Ty swore under his breath, but his father heard the soft expletive.

"Or maybe he hasn't learned, after all. Is that any kind of language to use at the dinner table?" Evans had obviously baited his son, and Ty had fallen for it.

"Excuse me, please." Ty stood, the chair scraping from behind him with a grating sound on the parquet floor. Throwing his napkin down across his unfinished meal, he left the room.

"Excuse my son's bad behavior, Miss Warren. I'm afraid he's never been able to control his temper. Lord knows we've tried everything to teach him otherwise. I suppose it falls to me to try again." Edward Evans stood then and followed his son from the room.

Stupified, Pam stared at the door through which they both departed. When her gaze traveled back to the table she found Marie Evans in tears. Compassion welled within her for the pitiful woman, and Pam went to her side of the table and put a gentle arm about her shoulders. A freshet of words poured from Mrs. Evans.

"I'd so hoped they would get along tonight. I thought it would be better with you here. Tyler has never been in this house longer than an hour since he moved out. Edward can't seem to leave him alone. He doesn't understand that the boy doesn't respond to his harsh disciplining. I'd hoped when he saw Ty as a man he'd quit hounding him. But he never does, Pam. He never does. . . ."

Pam held the older woman in her arms, and they rocked silently together. Pam began to realize that she had only seen the tip of the iceberg in a match of unending rounds between combatants. Whatever went on between Ty and his father was deeper and more troubled than she had ever dreamed.

Smoothing the damp curls off the older woman's brow, Pam suggested, "Why don't we go into the living room? I'm full already. Maybe we can coax them to join us for tea?"

Marie nodded hopefully and, dabbing at her eyes, led the way.

"Pam, would you tell the maid to bring tea? And pick whatever kind you prefer. Earl Grey is always nice. Or something fruity. I'll stoke the fire, and we'll pretend none of this ever happened."

Though she kept the thought to herself, Pam knew that Marie Evans was already denying what had gone on between her husband and her son. She was as weak as Ty had indicated—weak or frightened.

Unsure of her way to the kitchen, Pam turned in a hallway and came face to face with a closed door. Behind that door she could hear the voices of Ty and his father.

"How dare you speak that way to me? You're an ungrateful, uncouth worthless bum! You play games for a living when you could be doing a decent day's work. I'd have been better off if you'd never been born!"

Ty's response to his father's tirade was muffled, his back evidently facing the door, but Pam, staggered by the venom in Edward Evans' words, sank back against the wall, stunned.

The sound of a scuffle ensued and Pam straightened. A stranger or not, she couldn't let this family pummel itself to death in her presence. She grasped the doorknob and stepped into the room.

Edward Evans had a fireplace poker in one hand poised over Ty's head. But Ty, stronger and more agile, had his father's forearm in a crushing grip rendering the makeshift weapon useless. He was twisting his father's arm in an effort to make him drop the metal shaft.

From inside the room she could hear Ty's words. "You can't hit me any more, *Father*." The words were an angry curse. "I'm bigger than you are now. I know that's hard on you because it makes it difficult to bully me around. I'm not a little boy to be battered around like a punching bag every time I displease you. You see," and Ty's voice lowered menacingly, "I'm the powerful one now. Whatever spell you have woven around Mother doesn't work with me. You can't hurt me anymore. I've been hurt enough." With that Ty jerked on his father's arm, and the poker fell to the floor with a clatter.

Ty turned toward the door and saw Pam standing there, frozen to the spot. Unfathomable sadness welled in the golden eyes, and he spoke. "Come on, Pam. We're going now." And to his father who stood still breathing deeply from the exertion, "Merry Christmas, *Daddy*. It's been like all the others."

Unspeaking they raced down the corridor to the foyer. Ty pulled Pam's coat from its hanger and tossed it to her. She tugged it on as she followed him out the front door. He hadn't even taken time to put his own coat on. As she neared the car she could hear Marie Evans' voice, "You've done it again, haven't you Edward? Why can't you learn? Why can't you learn . . ."

Pam was trembling so from nerves and cold that her teeth chattered and her body shook. But for all her agitation, she was in a far better condition than Ty.

He threw his coat across the hood of the car and stood with his hands on the roof molding, palms down and was painfully, gut-wrenchingly sick. Finally he raised his head. He was pale as the moon-lit snow as he spoke. "Let's get out of here. I don't know why I tried coming back. It's always the same."

Pam nodded and asked timidly, "May I drive?" Ty looked in no shape to be behind the wheel.

He nodded and they pulled away from the imposing mansion shrouded in dark shadows. All the lights had gone off in the house, and Pam was reminded of a black hole in outer space, so vast and so dark that no light could escape.

She kept glancing at Ty as she drove, but he did not move. He had flung his head back against the seat and lay there unmoving. She could see every line of his finely chisled profile from the soft wave of hair on his forehead to the gentle rise of his Adam's apple. Only his ragged breath revealed he was human, not stone.

"Ty, we're at my apartment. Come inside." Pam cautiously touched the sleeve of his suitcoat.

"Are you sure you want me to?"

"Positive. I think you need to talk."

"I haven't talked to anyone about this in twenty-eight years. What makes you think tonight is a good time to start?" There was no rancor in his voice, only mild curiosity.

"You've waited too long already. Come on."

He followed her lead docilely, seemingly oblivious to the winter chill. He held the lush beaver coat behind him, the bottom third dragging on the ground. But Pam, now knowing how little the gift meant to the giver, couldn't force herself to chastise him.

"Tea? Coffee? Soda?"

"Got any whiskey?"

"You should know better than that by now."

"Coffee then." Ty spread himself across her couch, suitcoat and tie discarded on the floor.

Minutes later Pam brought a tray of mugs and crackers to his side. "Will this help?" she asked offering him the plate of dry crackers.

"Playing nursemaid?" he sounded almost amused. "This patient isn't exactly sick, you know. Let's just say I had an allergic reaction to a foul substance—my father."

"Ty, about your father—"

"What about him, Pam? You saw him in rare form tonight. He must be slipping with age. When I was a child he never attempted to beat me in public—bad for the image, I suppose. Of course, you weren't supposed to come toddling into the study either. Caught him off guard, you did. Hope it scared him." Ty stared into the bottom of the mug thoughtfully.

"It's always been like this, then?" Pam ventured.

"More or less. Except now I can fend him off. He's sick, Pam. Really sick. I know that now. As a child I thought *I* was the one who was sick or perverted. *I* was the one who couldn't ever get anything right or live up to his standards. It's a great way for a child to grow up, Pam. Be thankful for your own father. I'd trade in a minute."

"I'm so sorry."

"So am I, Prudish Pamela. I'm sorry you had to get in on our annual Christmas brawl. But now maybe you understand why I choose not to talk about my background. It would make ugly headlines if it came out—'Hockey Player Was Battered Child, Gets Revenge On Ice'—you know, that sort of thing." He stood in one fluid motion, scooping his clothing from the floor. "I gotta go, Pam. I need to think. I'm sorry about the night."

She nodded and stood with him. Shyly she ventured, "Ty, would you like to spend Christmas Eve with me? I've been invited to the Williamson's for dinner on Christmas Day, but I'll be alone tomorrow night. Unless, of course, you have somewhere else to go. . . ."

"Thanks, Pam. I'd like that. I doubt even my mother will attempt to get me over to the house again."

"Then come any time after five. I'll fix supper."

He nodded and came toward her unspeaking. Slipping his arm around her shoulders, he pulled her to him and held her close. Pam could feel the rhythmic

127

thudding of his heart and smell the tangy cologne he wore. Then she felt his cheek rest tenderly on the top of her head for a brief moment. He squeezed her gently and released her. Without speaking he walked out the door and into the night.

The dreadful time past, the adrenaline that had kept Pam upright stopped pumping, and she sank onto the couch. Finally she understood his silences. And his secrets bore the marks of a private hell she could not begin to understand. With knowledge came responsibility, for now Pam knew the intimate, personal world of Tiger Evans.

In an attempt to make up for the dreadful meal of the prior evening, Pam labored feverishly over her Christmas Eve dinner. Knowing a turkey would be foolish to cook for the two of them, she choose plump, fresh Cornish game hens stuffed with wild rice and almonds. She had even gone so far as to spend some of her gift money on a tiny tin of caviar. She was still spreading it on toast triangles when the doorbell rang.

"Merry Christmas!" Ty stood at the door looking like a lumberjack. He wore a red and black buffalo plaid flannel shirt and form fitting black jeans. Under one arm was tucked a large foil-wrapped box with a mammoth red bow. In the other was a tiny package wrapped in florist's paper.

"Merry Christmas to you! You're just on time. I'm finishing up the canapes."

"Canapes? I thought you lived the simple life back in Arizona?" He put the big box on the floor next to the door and began to unwrap the tiny one.

"But I read about canapes. I hope you like caviar because if you don't I'm in trouble. I'll have to attempt to string those little beads and wear them around my neck!"

"Don't go to the zoo smelling like a fish. You're

likely to be somebody's lunch—but don't worry. I'm crazy about caviar." Ty finished unwrapping the parcel and the paper drifted to the floor. Still he kept it from Pam's sight. Then, quickly, he lifted his arm into the air over her head and his lips came down upon hers claiming them with startling suddenness.

"Wha—Umm—" Pam struggled for a brief moment and then succumbed to the kisses. After a few moments she opened her eyes as she felt something light and feathery fall to her shoulder. She could see from the corner of her eye a spring of mistletoe balancing precariously.

"Ty Evans, you old fox!"

He grinned and tucked the mistletoe into his shirt pocket. "With you I feel like I need an excuse, Prudish Pamela. And now I have one, so look out!"

A sizzle of excitement burned deep within her. Pushing him away, she turned toward the kitchen. It didn't seem wise—or safe—to let Ty know how deeply he could affect her.

The burning warmth remained with her all evening. Sitting across from Ty, watching his features change with the flickering candlelight, she began to imagine how it would be if they were to do this every evening. And then she would remember his pain of the night before and the haunted, hunted look in his eyes. Ty Evans was meant to be free. Fettered, he might change into some prowling, unsettled sort. Whatever became of their relationship, she could put no demands on him. He had had enough of that to last a lifetime.

"You look rather serious, Pam. What's causing that glint in your eyes?" Ty inquired, swirling the dregs of his coffee in the bottom of the cup.

No demands. No traps. The thoughts blazed through her mind like a comet. Pulling herself together, Pam parried, "I was thinking about that big package you brought. Who is it for?"

"Who do you think? How could I come for Christmas Eve and not have a present for the hostess?"

"Well, I don't have anything that big for you."

"You don't have to have anything at all. I'd rather be the giver." Ty stretched backward in his chair, the thick muscles of his chest straining at the buttons of his shirt.

"Well, I'd hardly invite a guest for Christmas Eve and not have a present for him."

"Then I think we should take a look at these mysterious packages—or do we have to do dishes first?"

"Just leave them. I'll do them in the morning." Pam waved a careless hand at the cluttered kitchen.

"I think I want to help you do them. I'd feel a consuming guilt for the rest of the holiday if I didn't." Ty began stacking the plates and cups.

"Really, Ty, that's not necessary."

"So humor me. Come on." He headed for the kitchen.

Pam had never realized what a heady experience dishwashing could be. Ty insisted on blowing soap bubbles her way. Once a large shimmery bubble landed on her cheek, and he broke it with his lips and nuzzled deeply into her shoulder. Pam could feel his wet soapy hands kneading the soft hollows of her back, and somehow she didn't mind the thought of wet sloppy hand prints on the tunic she had chosen so carefully for this evening. Between the bubbles and the brief interludes when Ty seemed to forget his job as dishwasher and pursued the cook, it took them nearly an hour to have the galley kitchen cleaned and free of clutter.

"Well, thank you, Ty. But I'm not sure you'd be of much help on a day-to-day basis. I don't have three hours in my daily schedule to spend washing dishes!"

"Try and work it in. Then I'll buy you a dishwasher, and we can spend those three hours some other way." He came at her smiling and wrapped his hands gently about her waist.

Startled by the freshet of emotion she was experiencing, Pam grasped for a distraction.

"The presents! We almost forgot the presents!"

"What presents?" Ty's voice was muffled as it carried through the soft silk of her hair.

"The big one you brought and the little one I have for you."

He pulled away and studied her with a pleased expression in his eyes. "You mean you really do have one for me? That's nice, Pam."

A sudden stinging made her blink her eyelids rapidly. It was apparent that Ty wasn't used to getting gifts—other than expensive pacifiers sent impersonally from stores to his apartment. Pam wished she were sure he would like her gifts.

"Well, let's get on with it then. Can I open mine first?" Ty was like a five-year-old.

"I suppose." Pam reached in the end-table drawer and drew out two gifts, one tiny and square, the other rectangular.

"Two! I got two?" Ty weighed the gifts, one in each hand.

"Well, one I just wrapped this evening. I hadn't planned on giving it to you, and you may not like it. But I thought you needed it right now," Pam began apologizing, suddenly sorry for her impulsiveness. But it was too late now, for Tiger was not about to give one gift back.

He plopped onto the couch and placed both gifts before him. "Which one do I open first?"

"The little one."

"Okay." He flicked his fingernail along the seam of the wrap, carefully freeing the parcel from the paper.

"You can just rip and tear, Ty. I always do."

"I know. But maybe I'll want to save it. Could it be

131

that I'm more sentimental than you've given me credit for?" Ty teased, but a hint of truth rang in the words.

Deeply touched, Pamela sat down beside him to watch him open her gift. Carefully he lifted the velvety jeweler's box from its wrap. He fingered the softness for a moment before lifting the lid, smiling slightly. Nervous emotion nearly choked Pamela as she watched. She was increasingly aware that Ty had not received many gifts given in love.

Love. Was that how she had given her gift? More and more she was beginning to believe so—impossible love that could never be between a wealthy, famous hockey player with a scarred and shadowed background and herself, a simple, God-fearing pastor's child struggling to make a life as a writer.

"Pam!" The word was soft as a caress. Ty had opened the box and was staring at the golden tie tack inside. It had been far more expensive than anything for which she had budgeted, but when she had seen the tiny golden tiger's head with amber eyes, she could not resist. The look in Ty's eyes made up for all the weeks of hot dogs and beans she might face.

"Thank you." Pam sensed more appreciation in those two simple words than in a torrent of grateful praise.

"You're welcome." The last syllable of her response was muffled by Ty's lips as they captured her own. His physical response made her wish she had a room full of gifts with which to shower him.

Finally untwining himself, Ty shrugged slightly and said, "Enough of that or we'll never get to the other gifts. Now it's your turn."

Her eyes fell for a moment on the second package she had wrapped for Ty. He caught her eye and shook his head. 'Uh-uh. I'm saving that for last. I want to drag out the pleasure as long as I can."

But that may not please you. Pam bit her lip and kept her thoughts to herself. She might have ruined the end of the evening with her second gift, but it was too late to retreat now.

"Open it." Ty thrust the large package into Pam's lap. With a sense of nervous anticipation she tore at the bow with shaking fingers. Somehow, she sensed the gift would be a monumental one.

Squeezing her eyes shut, she lifted the top from the box. Then opening them only a slit, which grew rapidly into round-eyed amazement, she stared into the parcel. Inside a wisp of tissue packing was the most magnificent red fox coat she had ever seen. The billowy softness bloomed from its confines as she ran an exploratory finger across the fur.

"Ty, you shouldn't have. I can't take this. It's—"

"Pam!" The sharpness in Ty's voice brought her up short. "Don't ruin things, please. Take it. Enjoy it."

"But it cost too much—"

"Pam, what I paid for that coat isn't going to mean as much in my budget as that little gold tiger did in yours. In terms of sacrifice, you offered much more. You can understand that, can't you?"

Immediately Pam's mind raced to the Scripture, and she remembered the parable of the old woman giving her last two coins. Jesus had recognized the personal cost of the gift more than its monetary value. Was refusing the gift taking away the joy of the giver?

Pam smiled into the golden eyes that had become anxious. "Thank you, Tiger Evans. This is the most wonderful gift I've ever received."

The anxiety slipped away, and he smiled a room-illuminating smile. "That's better! Don't ever scare me like that again. Come on, try it on." He pulled the luxurious coat from the box and held it out for her to slip into. It settled around Pam's shoulders like a cloud.

Burying her nose in the fluffy collar, she murmured, "It's too much, you know. It really is."

"Remember, my father is a furrier. Whatever has

133

gone on between us, I can still go into his store and strike a bargain—because he wants it that way. I've almost come to terms with what he is, Pam. I used to think he hated me just because I existed. Now, with age, I'm beginning to think it's because I'm not fulfilling the dreams he had for himself. He's sick and he's hateful, but somewhere in that cauldron of malice he realizes that I am his son—his only son. He can't seem to deal with me on a personal level, but from a distance—a long distance," Ty chuckled ruefully, "we can cohabit the same Province. And I *can* shop in his stores."

Pam's chest labored under the threatening tears. Still, after what she had seen last night, Ty seemed willing to understand his father. There was more strength and compassion in the abused, rejected child than she could believe possible. Perhaps the second gift would be accepted after all—and in the manner in which it was given.

Silently, she took his hands and wrapped them around herself. Leaning a cheek against the soft flannel of his shirt, she wept. For him. For herself. For the generosity he had shown.

"Hey! You're going to cry yourself right out of getting presents! I could have bought a jug of 'toilette water' at the five-and-dime, and the smell would have kept you in tears for a year! Cheer up!" Ty chucked her under the chin and pushed her away from himself. "Anyway, I think you're just trying to keep me from the other package. And it's not going to work."

Still snuffling but beginning to chuckle, Pam retorted, "Maybe we should save that for another day. I've had about as much emotion as I can take for one evening."

He gave her a quizzical glance. "Emotion? You mean there's something emotional about this?" He weighed the parcel in his palm.

"Ty, maybe I should explain—"

"Before or after I open it?"

"Both. I wrapped this on impulse, Ty. Don't be angry. It's something that means a great deal to me, and I want it to mean as much to you—please don't feel I'm pushing you, but after last night . . ."

All the levity was gone from his voice. "Then maybe I'd better open this Pamela, and see what you're talking about." Obviously the mention of last night had put the brakes on his anticipation.

Opening the second package with the same care as the first, Ty allowed the wrapping to fall away. Left in his hands was a tattered Bible. In the lower right hand corner, in golden letters nearly worn away were the words "Pamela Warren."

"Ty—"

"But this is yours, Pam!" His brow furrowed in confusion.

"I know. But I thought you needed it. It was a reward for perfect attendance in Sunday School that I received as a child. It's all underlined, and I've scribbled thoughts in the margins, but maybe that will help you understand. I have several others, but I traveled my path through the Scriptures first when I was a child. That's a good way to accept what it says—with childlike openness. Maybe my childish scrawls, my teenage questions, and my adult thoughts will help you. Please don't be offended that I've given you something so battered and old."

"Offended? How could I be offended by receiving something you value so much?"

He understood! But Pam's relief was short-lived.

"But it's useless, Pam. I don't see how the words in here can mean anything to me. What I treasure is the thought that you'd share something you've loved with me. I can't take anything you value so much away from you." He offered the book to her.

Silently she stood and removed the cloak of fur. Holding it out to him she said, "Then I can't take this

135

from you. These are gifts, Ty, meant to be used and enjoyed. If you can't take mine, I can't take yours."

Ty glanced for a minute at the book in his hands. "Okay. I'll take it—and I'll read it. Now will you keep the coat?" He looked up at her much like a child outsmarted at play.

"As long as you keep the Bible." Pam began to smile.

"Deal. I'm glad you don't play hockey. If you acted like this on the ice, I'd never have a chance."

Pam grinned momentarily, but was still not satisfied that Ty understood her purpose. "Ty, after what I saw at your house last night, I know more than ever that you need strength and the capacity to love. Take the words seriously. There are answers in there for questions you haven't even thought to ask yet."

"I will, Pam. I promise." The dark golden flickering of his eyes proved his solemnity. Then they brightened, and he added, "I'd be the laughing stock of the team if I got that coat back and had to wear it to practice!"

"Araghh!" Pam bleated and dived at him pummeling him on the chest. He grinned and wrapped his arms about her, and they fell back onto the couch. Content, they held each other in warm, companionable silence.

"Ty?" Pamela ventured, hesitantly breaking the cozy quietude.

"Hmm?"

"Do you want to go to church with me tonight?"

Pam found herself sliding undecorously to the floor. Ty's face bent even with hers, and he put his index finger under her chin. "You don't give up for a minute, do you?"

"Not when it means a great deal to me. Tonight is Christmas Eve!"

He uttered a resigned sigh. "You're right. Maybe it would be good for me. I can't remember going to church on Christmas Eve since I was eight years old."

"Then come tonight. Please?"

"I don't know what kind of power you hold over me, Prudish Pamela, but all right. Just this *once*."

Delighted, Pam jumped to her feet. "Then let's go!"

"Isn't it awfully cold to be running out like this?" Ty hedged, still lounging on the couch.

"Not a bit. I want to try out my new coat."

A groan emanated from the divan. "I've created a monster! Give it back!"

"No chance. We made a deal. Here's yours." Pam threw the coat over his shoulder and opened the door. There was going to be no stopping her tonight.

The church was shrouded in darkness as they entered. Pam recognized Wendy's light touch at the organ keyboard and the dear, familiar Christmas tunes echoing through the sanctuary. She headed toward the front only to find herself jerked back by Ty's restraining hand.

"Not in front." There was a nervousness in his voice she had not heard before.

Nodding, she slipped into a back pew. If this is where he would be comfortable, it was fine with her.

The service was a simple one, replete with familiar carols and a moving reading of the Christmas story. As they sat, holding lit candles in the darkened church and singing the final strains of "Silent Night," Pam glanced at Ty.

He had an odd, thoughtful look on his face. He turned toward her as though he had felt her gaze resting on him. He smiled and mouthed a single word to her, "Thanks."

Finally assuaged, Pam settled against the wooden pew. She had done all she could to offer Ty the peace and joy she knew. Now she would pray for her heavenly Father to do the rest.

They rode to Pam's apartment in silence. It was not until they reached her door that Ty commented. "That was nice. Nicer than I thought."

"Good. I'm sorry I'm such a demanding sort."

"That's okay. I'm getting used to it. You've caused me extra work and trouble since the moment we met. I've come to expect it."

Pam punched him playfully in the arm, but, undaunted, Ty made his way into the apartment and toward the kitchen. "Is there any of that pumpkin pie left?" He was foraging in the refrigerator.

"There should be a half a pie somewhere. I ate one slice and you ate two."

"Care to join me?" Ty had the pie tin in one hand and a quart of ice cream in the other.

"Why not? This is a special occasion. Once my waistline begins to grow, you'll have to eat it all yourself."

Ty ogled her tiny waist appreciatively. "Don't worry. I can keep track of what you eat by how my hand fits around your middle. One fingernail's breadth larger, and I'll put my foot down."

They sat side by side at Pam's tiny dining room table and looked out at the panorama of the city. Ty rose once to flick off the lights, and they stared at the unending strings of lights that meandered off into the prairie surrounding the city.

Ty's arm found its way around Pam's shoulders, and she rested her head against him. Their breathing rose and fell harmoniously in the darkened room. Soon she felt his lips nuzzling deeply in her hair and a warm glow began to build within her. She didn't struggle when Ty stood and picked her up, one arm around her back, the other under her knees and carried her to the couch.

He wound exploring fingers in the waterfall of her hair, and his lips surveyed the curves and angles of her face. In the quiet, Pam could hear his breath grow ragged and feel the passion of his kisses increase.

138

"Pam?" He left the rest of the question unasked, but Pamela knew its meaning.

He wanted to stay. And she could not deny that she wanted it too, but her resolve firm, she whispered, "You have to go now, Ty. Please?"

He lifted his head, and all she could see in the darkness were the burning embers of reflected light in his golden eyes. He blinked, catlike, and his lips came down upon hers once again.

This time, with more resoluteness, she pushed at his shoulders. "*Now*, Ty."

Expelling a ragged breath, he shifted on the couch. "Are you sure, Pam?"

"Very sure. And thank you for the most wonderful evening of my life."

Unwillingly he stood. "I'll leave tonight, Pam, because I don't want to ruin anything. But I don't want to. And some night I won't. Remember that."

She watched him draw on his coat and pick up the two small packages she had given him. He bent low to kiss her good night. His lips grazed hers, tracing a pattern of scorching heat across them. Soundlessly he left the darkened room, closing the door behind him until all that remained was the slash of light from the hallway at the threshold.

Pam sighed and leaned her head against the couch, her hair cascading over the rim like tears.

CHAPTER 8

PAM GRIPPED THE WHEEL of her car until her knuckles turned white with exertion. She should never have agreed to do a story out of the city, unaccustomed as she was to winter driving. The familiar black and white ribbons of ice and pavement of Winnipeg were gone. The road bed was no where to be seen under the sheet of ice she was traversing. Blowing snow swirled beneath her tires like Arizona dust devils. She felt as though she were trying to find a white kitten in a flour bin as the ground blizzard increased around her. The first traces of fear were beginning to gnaw at her midsection.

She sought a mental distraction from the whirling, swirling snow and precarious ice beneath her. She began to speak aloud, softly at first and then with more intensity, comforted by the sound of her own voice.

"Ty! I'll think about Ty!" she announced to herself. "Oh, Ty! I wish you were here right now!"

Christmas had passed and Ty left the city on the twenty-sixth for an extended road trip. It was because her days had seemed so empty and her nights so long that she had agreed to cover a high-school hockey tournament in an outlying hamlet.

"He should be back soon," she announced to the rear-view mirror, which pictured only more of the swirling white powder. "Maybe today or tomorrow. I wish he had called—and maybe I wouldn't have left town." Her voice cracked on that note, and she gave a shivery sob. She dared not turn around for if there were vehicles behind her they would surely run her over. And she dared not continue, but there seemed no other choice.

Suddenly her rear wheels began to skid. Pam recalled the words of caution Ty had given her before he left. "Now be careful on the ice, Pam. You aren't used to it, and accidents can happen very quickly. If you start to skid, don't panic, don't jerk the steering wheel, and whatever you do, don't step on the brakes. Turn into the skid until you have the car under control, then turn the direction you want to go. Sounds crazy, but it works."

As her car came out of the skid, Pam reiterated his words, "Crazy, but it works!" Limbs watery with relief, Pam loosened her stranglehold on the steering wheel for a moment and peered through the sweep of windshield. Whiteness. Solid, blank whiteness.

Thunk. . Her vigil relaxed for only a moment, she had lost her way on the pavement and driven over the edge into the ditch. Pushing the gas pedal to the floor rewarded her only with the loud, lunging noises of the entrapped vehicle.

Panicking, she began to rock the car back and forth, slipping the gears from low to reverse and back again. The engine roared but to no avail. Finally seeing the fruitlessness of the act, Pam stopped, realizing too late that perhaps all she had done was dig the car in even deeper.

Stranded!

Taking stock of the situation, Pam again recalled Ty's warning words. "Never leave a car if you get stuck. Stay with the vehicle. Especially if it's snowing. You have winter gear in the trunk. Get it out. Wrap up. Run the car for a few minutes every half hour to keep yourself warm. Roll the window down a crack on the downwind side for fresh air. You'll be okay as long as you don't panic."

Suddenly the part about not panicking seemed hardest of all. Pam methodically followed Ty's instructions as she remembered them, grateful for the time he had taken with her.

Piling her winter survival kit into the front seat, Pam crawled in after it. The sleeping bag was icy cold as she snuggled her legs and feet into the fleece, but she soon felt it warming as she rubbed her legs against the lining.

She was most grateful of all for the coat Ty had given her as she wrapped it tightly about herself. The fur broke the wind and held her body heat in a cozy cocoon.

"Don't panic, Pam. Stay calm." She took a series of deep breaths in an attempt to quiet her pounding heart. Then, knowing full well what serious trouble she was in, she bowed her head and prayed.

The hours passed with interminable slowness. Each elapsing moment dashed further her hope that the violent blizzard would subside. At noon Pam noticed a new brightness in the snow. Startled, she looked up. Through the whirling whiteness she could see the sun. She had been on the road for three hours.

A tear dripped down one cheek and poised immobile there. Daylight would diminish with each passing hour now and her hopes for rescue that day would dwindle as well. The gauge of her gas tank was dropping. She dared to run it less and less with each fleeting hour. Would this be where she spent the last hours of her life?

How ironic. She could imagine the headlines now. "Arizona Woman Found Frozen in Countryside." Of all the dangers her father had warned, even he hadn't imagined this one.

Resigned and dreadfully weary, Pam found herself drifting off to sleep.

"Pam? Pam! Are you in there?"

She was dreaming, of course. She was dreaming that Ty's voice was speaking to her. But it was muffled by something. What? Snow, perhaps. That accursed snow even infiltrated her dreams and muffled his beloved voice. Sleepily she buried herself deeper in the wonderful fox coat. *Leave me alone, snow. Let me dream of Ty.*

"Pamela Warren! If you're in there, speak to me!" The voice held a note of terror now. Suddenly the car shook and the door was wrenched open. Pamela fell backward into Tiger Evans' arms.

"Thank God you're alive!"

Still groggy and convinced she would never be rescued, Pam's first thoughts were, "Yes, indeed. Thank God!"

"Pam, talk to me."

It *was* Ty. It wasn't a dream. The nightmare was over. "Ty?"

"Yeh, Pam, it's Ty." His voice shook with relief. Though the circle of his arms never left her, he turned and called over his shoulder, "It's her, and she's okay. She's cold, but she's alive."

Pam felt herself being pulled unceremoniously from her car and wrapped in Ty's arms. He carried her to the cab of a large snow plow and lifted her to the man inside.

She felt like a doll being tossed about and oddly enough when she finally felt the warmth of the gusting heater, she began to shiver uncontrollably. She heard herself asking questions in an unfamiliar voice—vague, slow, and slurred.

"Hey, Tiger. I think she's suffering from hypothermia. Come and listen to her talk." The driver of the snow plow was yelling through a crack in his window. Exhausted, Pam wished he would be quiet so she could sleep.

She felt Ty swing into the cab.

"She's got the car dug in deep. We'll send a wrecker for it when it clears up. Let's get her back into town. How's she acting?" Ty loosened the top clasp of her coat and ran his fingers around the neck of her sweater.

"Shivering, slurred speech, sleepy. I think we'd better get her to a doctor."

Ty nodded in agreement and asked, "Is there anything in that thermos?"

"Hot coffee. Think you can get her to drink some?"

"I'd better try. I don't know what else to do for hypothermia." He lifted her head, and Pam felt a sizzling warmth slide across her tongue. She sputtered, and her eyes flew open as Ty laughed. "Now you did it, Pam. You spilt coffee all over my jacket. Is that any way to say thank you to the guy who rescued you?"

"My knight on a shining snow plow . . ." Ty let her doze off again in his arms, but the doctors and nurses at the hospital were less accommodating.

Pam was feeling almost normal and a bit embarrassed by the time Ty walked into her hospital room and began to chuckle at the unbecoming sack of a gown that kept slipping off her shoulder.

"Hi, fashion plate. Where'd you get the fancy dress?"

"Don't tease, Ty. I'm embarrassed enough as it is. Why won't they let me leave with you?"

"Patience, Miss Priss. You can go in the morning. You're here for 'observation.' Although I think I could do a perfectly good job of it at your apartment, they don't trust me." Ty slid a hip onto the bed and began toying with her toes under the blankets.

"I'm not even sure what happened to me!"

"In a nutshell, your body began to lose heat faster than it could produce it. I think it's those Arizona genes—no stamina bred into you. But you've warmed up and will be just fine."

"How did you find me, Ty? I didn't even know when you'd be back in town." The import of what he had done was finally dawning on her. He had probably saved her life.

"We got in on a nine o'clock flight this morning. I took my luggage home and gave you a call at the office. They told me you'd taken off for some little town to the west. Well, I yelled at whoever was on the phone for a while, asking them why they were fools enough to let you start out in weather like this. Then I went to look for you myself. It got too thick to even leave the city limits so I turned around and looked up an old friend of mine."

"The man in the snow plow?" Pam's fingers had found Ty's at the middle of the bed.

"Yup. I went to high school with him. He was supposed to be going out anyway so I hitched a ride. And found you." Sitting at the foot of her bed, he looked big and cozy and more dear than anyone she had ever known. His hair was longer and curled at his collar but those days apart had not changed the look in his eyes—or the love she was beginning to feel for him.

"You go to sleep now, Pam. I'm going to stop and say hi to Brock Madsen before I go home. Your boss says you have the rest of the week off. I'll pick you up at check-out time."

"Ty,' Pam willingly snuggled into the pillow, "how is he?"

A length of silence met her.

145

"Ty?"

"He's going to be blind, Pam. There's nothing they can do."

"Oh, Ty!" She sat up in the bed but felt warm gentle hands pushing her backward.

"Don't think about it tonight, Pam. I'll answer your questions tomorrow if you'd like. Please."

As much as Pam wanted to think of Ty's friend and his suffering, an overwhelming tiredness thwarted her. She was asleep before Tiger left the room.

"Hi, Miss Priss! You look better today!" Ty sauntered in, swinging a shopping bag.

"I'm glad you think so. I feel like warmed-over toast."

"Yuk!" he grimaced, "That sounds terrible! Here maybe this will help."

Pam peeked into the bag he tossed on the bed. Inside was a set of clothing. Chocolate-brown wool slacks and a honey-colored sweater just the color of Ty's eyes. "Ty! They're lovely! But why?"

"I didn't think you'd want to wear your other clothing today. I don't have a key to your apartment so I went out and bought you some. Did I get the size right?"

Gratefulness surged through her again. He never seemed to run out of ideas to make her feel good. "I really do appreciate this, Ty. They should fit perfectly. I'll pay you back."

"You do that. I'll tell you when I want to collect."

She glanced at him curiously, but he returned her stare blandly, whatever innuendo was hidden in his words was not about to be explained.

She banished him to the hallway and slipped into the garments. They were far more expensive than any she ever purchased for herself. Ty did everything on a grander scale than she was accustomed to.

"Decent?" He poked his head around the door.

146

"Yes. Come in."

Ty strolled in and a white-garbed doctor followed him.

"So you're ready to go home today?" the physician inquired.

"Yes. And as soon as possible. I've had enough adventures and out-of-the-ordinary things for a long time."

"My advice is that you avoid ditches in blizzards, Miss Warren. Other than that you can proceed normally." The doctor scratched his name onto her chart.

"What about hot tubs?" Ty inquired from his post at the doorway.

"What about them?"

"Can she be in one? I have to work out at my health club today. I'd like to take her along and keep an eye on her. Can she sit in the hot tub?"

"That sounds like a fairly innocuous activity." The physician turned to Pam. "You're very lucky to have him watching out for you, Miss Warren."

She nodded in mute agreement. *Very* lucky!

"Let's stop by your apartment and pick up a swimsuit and then go to the club." Ty pulled into the ten-minute parking space before her building.

"Really, Ty. You don't have to baby me like this. I'll be fine at home."

"Quite arguing. Do you want to give me the key and tell me where it is or would you rather go in yourself?"

"Give me five minutes." Pam dashed from the car to the doorway. She really didn't want to spend the day at home alone anyway.

The clanking of weights met them at the door of the club. Ty pushed her gently toward the ladies' locker room.

"Meet me at the weight room whenever you're ready. I'll take you in to see the pools. Go on." He urged her away, laughing at her hesitance and called after her, "Don't be shy, Prudish Pamela. Everyone here wears a swimming suit!"

It was odd, Pam decided, to be slipping into a swim suit when it was blustery and cold outside. All her swimming had been done in outdoor pools—summer and winter. She slipped the teal crinkle-knit suit over her hips and tugged it up under her arms. The brief ruffle that encased the elastic and held the suit in place tickled her slightly as she moved her arms. Her father had looked askance at a strapless suit, but it had been the most concealing in the store. After a foray into bikinis the size of knee patches, the crinkly teal had seemed almost subdued.

Grabbing her towel she went in search of Ty.

He was in the weight room laying on his back doing bench presses. Already sweat was pouring off his forehead, and dark lines of moisture followed the hollows of his body and soaked through his T-shirt. Pam noticed that the pin was set deeply in the stack of weights. Ty must have been pressing nearly two hundred and fifty pounds. Her mind still fought translating kilograms into pounds.

"Hi." He tilted his head backward and looked at her upside down. His eyes widened appreciatively as they traveled from her thonged feet to the ruffle at the top of her suit and down again. Pam felt a blushing heat bleed across her face and shoulders.

"I can hardly wait for summer if that's what's under all those clothes." Ty rolled off the bench and stood up.

Self-consciously Pam wrapped her towel around her shoulders and noticed the disappointment in Ty's eyes. It was obvious that he was accustomed to women far more bold than she.

"Come on, Prudish Pamela. Let's find a place where you have no excuse to hide behind that towel and ruin the scenery." Ty held out a hand and led her toward the pool area.

Walking through big glass doors, they entered a humid arena. A large swimming pool occupied most of the space but one corner was cordoned off for whirlpools. Several swimmers were doing laps in the big pool but the whirlpools were sparsely populated.

"Hop in here, Pam. I'm going to swim some laps. Then I'll join you."

She nodded, dropped the towel from about her shoulders and slid quickly into the roiling water. Ty's eyes upon her made her uneasy. She didn't want him to get any more ideas than he already had.

Pam watched Ty swim laps from her perch in the whirlpool. She could see his smooth golden arms lift and lower rhythmically in the water. He glided like a fish, spun, kicked himself off the edge of the pool and swam back. He must have gone several miles by the time he stepped from the water and padded her way, shaking himself like a wet puppy.

"How does it feel?" He slid in beside her, his leg brushing her shoulder as he descended.

"I'm getting warm. I think I'll take a shower and dress."

"Leaving already?" His hand searched for hers under the water.

Purposefully avoiding it, she stood, put her hips on the rim of the tub and swung her legs out of the water. "It takes me a while to dry my hair, Ty. I'll meet you out front."

She could feel his amused gaze burning a pattern into her back as she escaped to the locker room. He was becoming more and more difficult to put off. If only he could grow to understand her! It was becoming clear that he would eventually expect of her what she knew she would save for marriage. And Tiger Evans gave no signs of being the marrying kind.

It was snowing again. Pam glanced out the health-club windows at the fluffy white flakes. Ty was

149

certainly taking a long time to get dressed. Then she noticed his gear stacked against the front desk. If he was already out of the locker room, where was he?

Again she went to the window to look toward his car. On the sloping rise behind the parking lot she saw Ty, stamping a pattern in the snow. Curious, she dropped her own bag and went to find out what he was doing. As she neared the hillside, tears began to sting at the backs of her eyes.

In the fresh white snow Ty had stamped a big heart. Now, head down, he was in the middle of the heart crushing the snow beneath his feet into words. Two words. "Pam—Ty." Intent on his work, he did not hear the crunchy warning of her footsteps. Only when she cleared her throat did he look up.

"You caught me."

"Even if I hadn't, I might have guessed who did it." The day felt like summer, so warm was the glow of pleasure Pam experienced. Ty grinned that endearing, heart-wrenching grin that brought the golden fleck to his eyes and Pam felt pangs of bittersweet happiness that brought her close to tears.

In that moment came the dawning realization of the love she had for him. And the fruitlessness of that love if Ty could not share her love of the Lord with her. She could not tear herself asunder—serving God and loving a man who couldn't understand that call.

Pain and joy mingled within her. Unless Ty grew to share her faith, she would have to make a choice. And that choice would not include the irreverent golden man she loved so deeply.

CHAPTER 9

"ARE YOU READY TO GO?" A frosty, snow-covered Ty stood before her, stamping his feet on the crusty ground.

"Oh, what? Yes." Pam gathered her bittersweet thoughts and smiled into his eyes. "Don't forget the gear."

Pam slipped into the little sports car and leaned her head back on the cushions. Things were moving far too rapidly for her. She hadn't meant to fall in love. And when she did, she had imagined it to be far different. She had always thought it would happen for her as it was for Wendy and Wendell. Shy people, similar in so many ways, learning to know each other gradually. Wendy had confided that their relationship was deepening—mentally and spiritually. She had said nothing of the physical. And Ty was *all* physical. But that was his life.

He slammed into the car, heaving the bags across the seat to the back. "Well, that should get me set for the road. I always like to swim and loosen up before a trip."

"When do you leave?" Relief and regret mingled in Pam's thoughts at the idea of Ty's departure on a road trip.

"Tonight. But we'll be back for a home game this weekend. A big one, too. That, plus this trip, could make or break us in the standings. We've all got to skate our best."

"Don't you always?" Pam asked curiously.

"Sure. But sometimes it's worth taking a few risks. Other times it's not."

"Risks?" A knot built in Pam's throat. She had heard those words once before—from Michael. And the risks hadn't been worth taking.

"Don't sound so alarmed. Skate a little harder, think a little faster, that's all. You act like I do high-beam construction for a living, not skating. Within five years I'll probably be sitting behind a desk somewhere, using my business degree and lifting weights to keep a paunch off my belly. Loosen up, Pam."

"And what about Brock Madsen? Would he tell you to loosen up?"

"Keep him out of this, Pam. What's with you today anyway?" Pam heard irritation in Ty's voice.

"Sorry."

"Okay." He turned and smiled, forgiving her for undue concern. "What are you going to do while I'm gone?"

"Work. Work. Work. And I promise to do it all within the city limits."

"Good girl. It's a long way from Edmonton to drag you out of a snow bank. Keep safe—okay?" His voice softened, and he touched her cheek with the back of his hand.

She nodded mutely but her mind screamed: *You keep safe Tiger Evans! You're the one who flirts with danger!*

The week without Ty was a tedious one. The

152

evening hours seemed endless when no one burst through her door suggesting dinner or swimming. By Saturday evening Pam was anxiously anticipating the match. It would be her first chance to see Ty since his return. Even under all that bulky equipment and baggy clothing, he would be a welcome sight.

Excitement snapped and sparkled like electricity within the arena. Ty had been right. This *was* to be a special game. Pam could feel it in the air. The road trip had been a successful one. All they needed was this game on home ice to secure a spot on the top. Pam edged her way to the press box and took a seat near Rick, her associate from the *Star*.

"Hi, Pam. Here for the big game, I see." Rick shot her that curious glance he always gave her when she attempted to be nonchalant about her relationship with Tiger Evans.

"Wouldn't miss it." She settled next to him, her eyes never leaving the still empty ice.

"I suppose these road trips get to be long for you too."

"Rick, I know what you're getting at, but, please, just leave it alone!"

"Come on, Pam! You know Tiger Evans better than anyone else I've ever known! With the Blazers on a winning streak, there couldn't be a more perfect time for some big story on his personal life. It would really get the fans going."

"I'm not about to use my personal influence with Ty to get a story that would please you, Rick."

"So don't *ask* him for a story! Just *do* one!"

"Our personal conversations are off the record, Rick."

"Leave it to Evans to cover every base. He doesn't even date without making sure it's off the record!"

Pam shot her co-worker a venomous look before returning her gaze to the ice. She wouldn't let him ruin her evening. Seeing Ty play was too precious for that.

"You know, I never realized until I tried to skate how difficult hockey must be. I hadn't even considered that a skater had to move with his head up at all times to avoid body checks and swinging sticks," Pam commented to Rick, remembering how difficult she found it to keep her eyes off the ice while she skated. Only Ty's golden eyes had pulled her away from her blades, stumbling along on the ice.

"And still manage to control the puck at the end of a stick?"

"Right." Pam chuckled as the first of the skaters poured into the arena. "I don't know how they perform at all under all those pieces of protective equipment."

"I read somewhere that hockey is the fastest team sport—the most difficult to play or watch. Do you agree?" Rick flipped open his notebook as the visiting team began to reconnoiter on the ice.

"Well, I'm just going to keep my eye on one player tonight, Rick. Hopefully I can manage that." Just then she saw Ty skate onto the ice. Even under all the equipment she could have recognized him—by the confident square of his shoulders and by the roar of the crowd that loved him almost as much as she did. He raised his stick in the air in a friendly hello and the crowd went wild. Tiger Evans was home.

He was graceful, agile and powerful on the ice. Skating with his knees slightly bent, his weight was always moving forward. Keeping his skates close to the ice and moving with long, smooth strides, Ty's skating looked effortless. But he could generate great power with strong hip action as he skated. He seemed more at ease on the vast expanse of slick ice than he did on solid earth, maintaining his balance with legs spread well apart. Effortlessly he began to skate backward, changing direction instantly. Pam forgave him for showing off a bit. This was his night to shine.

From the very first face-off the game was in high gear. Ty had the puck on his stick and was thwarting the opposition's attempts to take it away from him with adroit stick handling. He kept the puck moving with deft motions of the stick, working to set up a goal-scoring opportunity. Head held high, he kept his eyes on the situation in front of him. Pam knew if he looked toward the ice he would be knocked down and lose possession of the puck.

"Rick! Why is he doing that? Oh!" Pam's question was interrupted by Ty's crisp, sharp pass to another player, but Rick leaned over with an explanation.

"You mean why was he moving the puck from front to back on his stick?"

She nodded. It seemed rather sloppy and out of character considering Ty's ability.

"Because he's good. He had control of the puck all the time. It just didn't look like it. That kind of stick handling lures the opponents into a false sense of security. He thinks you're about to lose the puck, and just as he makes his move to take it off your stick, you react and retrieve the puck, sweeping it back and moving off—just like Tiger did right there. Duped him good."

Pam was dizzy by the end of the first period. The speed and continuous movement on the ice made even the spectator's job a demanding one. She wondered idly how Ty was doing down in the dressing room.

"Good game." Rick commented as he offered to share his box of popcorn.

"It seems rougher tonight than usual." Pam reached into the box and took a handful of kernels.

"More penalties. Everyone is on edge. That holding penalty was a stupid one to have to take."

"Why?" Pam was grateful for Rick's presence. He seemed so willing to explain the intricacies of the game. All her studying still couldn't match the knowledge of a life-long fan.

155

"Holding is always a stupid penalty to take. Grabbing an opposing player for just a second rarely incurs a penalty. Doing it obviously or for any length of time usually does. The best defensemen are masters of tying up a rival player without making a spectacle of it."

"Tempers seem to be flaring. I've never seen a slashing penalty called before tonight."

Rick nodded and dug deeper into the popcorn. "Highly-charged atmosphere. That's one thing about Tiger. He normally plays a clean game. He usually doesn't get tripped up with a lot of penalties. He could be pretty mean if he wanted to be. He's a big guy."

The second period only intensified the electric atmosphere. One of the opponents was thrown into the penalty box for cross-checking when he held his stick at each end and rammed into a Blazer. Having a player advantage, the Blazers scored on the power play, and the fans went berserk.

Pam, feeling the tension knotting at the back of her neck, glanced downward toward the ice just below her. Some young boys, the oldest of which couldn't have been more than ten, were tossing coins in the air at their seats. It was as if the events of the next few moments were movie stills flipped by Pam's eyes in slow motion.

She saw the bright glint of a copper penny arc in the air—higher, higher, higher. It sailed over the protective glass and onto the ice where it shimmered in the bright lights. No one but the boys and Pam seemed to have seen the errant penny sail away. But within seconds the entire arena knew something was amiss as a Blazer wing skated over it. The smooth stride broken he lost his balance and slammed uncontrollably into the boards. A communal gasp rose from the crowd, hovered in the air and died.

"Get up!" Pam heard herself scream at the prone skater. "Get up!"

But the broken body on the ice didn't move. Pam felt a sickening gorge rise in her throat as they carried the unconscious man from the ice, his teammates all milling around the stretcher helplessly. She couldn't pick Ty from the rest anymore without searching for the bold number on the back of his shirt. The assured carriage that set him apart from the rest was gone.

The game finished in a subdued fashion with a flurry of careless off-sides and sloppy play.

"Well, the Blazers won, but I wonder how much it's going to cost them." Rick tossed the comment out casually as he shrugged into his jacket.

"What do you mean by that?" Pam forced herself to move slowly, knowing that Ty wouldn't be at their meeting place for several minutes yet.

"From the looks of that tumble, the Blazers may be out another player for the rest of the season. First Brock Madsen, now this. The casualty list is growing."

Pam swallowed, willing away the sick feeling in her midsection. Ty had been skating close to his downed teammate. It could have been Ty unconscious on the ice. This time the fear she had been battling made headway against her resistance.

She met him in the long concrete hallway that led to the parking lot. He came walking toward her, head down, shoulders slumped, feet dragging.

"Hi."

He looked up, not even attempting a smile. "Hi." That copper penny had injured more than one party in its short stay on the ice.

"How is he?"

"He didn't regain consciousness before the ambulance left." Ty was watching her. She could feel his eyes travel over the planes of her face, studying her reaction.

She felt an overwhelming urge to throw up. Ty's

supportive hand at the small of her back kept her in control, and the sharp, chilly slap of the night air cleared her head.

"Ty, we have to talk."

"Your place or mine?"

"Mine." She hadn't planned it like this. She had envisioned running into his arms after their week apart, celebrating a joyous reunion. She had hoped for a quiet dinner somewhere with roses on the table and a single violin playing in the background. Instead, all the joy of their meeting had been banished by a copper penny and an unconscious skater.

Neither spoke until they were into her apartment. Ty dropped his coat on the floor beside the door while Pam hung hers away. She felt suddenly self-conscious and unfamiliar with him. The easy camaraderie of prior weeks had been stripped away. He sat down on the couch stiffly, rested his elbows on his knees, and hung his head toward the floor.

Pam silently heated two mugs of hot chocolate and carried them to the table beside him.

Finally, he spoke. "How was your week?"

"Quiet, without you. My desk is clean, and I'm three interviews ahead of myself. How was your week?"

"Fine, until tonight. Blast!" He threw himself back against the couch so that it shuddered. "What a stupid accident!"

'All accidents are stupid, Ty."

"Some more than others." He rubbed his forehead with the palm of his hand in a frustrated, scrubbing motion. Then he brightened slightly and added, "It's good to see you, Pam."

"It could have been you."

"What?" Ty's brow creased in confused furrows.

"That accident could have happened to you," she persisted.

"But it didn't."

"You were skating only a few feet behind him. If he'd missed it, you might have hit it."

"And if God gave pigs wings, then they could fly," Ty retorted. "I didn't hit it. That's what counts!"

"I don't like all these accidents, Ty. They scare me!"

"And do you think I enjoy them? It's part of the game, Pam. You take the good with the bad."

"You've played hockey for a long time."

"Most of my life. Why?"

"Isn't it almost time to give it up?" Pam hardly dared breathe the question she had been formulating in her mind all evening.

"Give it up? Why?" He looked at her in stunned amazement.

The reasons she had prepared all rushed from her in a gush. "You're one of the oldest players on the Blazers team. I know twenty-eight isn't old, but professional hockey teams seem to be getting younger and younger. . . ." Pam hardly dared continue as she saw the storm clouds brewing on Ty's face. "And you've never had a serious injury! Why don't you get out before you do? Look at Madsen. What did hockey do for him? Make him blind, that's what! And Ty, you have a wonderful education! You could be making your way in business right now instead of playing games. Think of it!" And her voice finally trailed away as the real reason for her pleadings was uttered, "I don't want you hurt, Ty. I've lost one friend. I can't bear to think of losing you."

"How did you lose a friend, Pam?" Ty's voice was soft, inquiring. Perhaps he had taken her plea in the spirit she had intended.

"He was a race-car driver. He saw his friends get hurt, but he always said he was lucky. Lucky! I watched him drive the day he died." Pam's voice trailed away.

Ty stood up and began to pace about the room.

"Pam, I understand why you're worried about me. But hockey and race cars are two entirely different things! One *is* dangerous—and it's not hockey! You can't ask me to give up what I love! What do you think kept me going all these years? It certainly wasn't my loving home life! What makes you think you can ask this of me?"

Pam felt a protective shutter fall. He wouldn't quit. So it was up to her to remove herself from the source of pain. She found herself pulling away—emotionally, physically. And she bit her lip to stop the answer to his question. But it screamed like a siren in her mind. *Because I love you!* A shadow had been cast over their relationship, a shadow of danger and fear. Was that shadow too dark and impenetrable to be broken by the light of love?

Ty seemed to sense the difference in her demeanor almost immediately. He stepped toward her, but the look in her face warned him away.

"All right, Pamela. If this is the way you want it. Make me choose between you and hockey. But I have to choose the game. It's my life. You won't let me get close enough to you to make it an honest choice. I can't even spend one night with you. At least hockey fills my days. I should have known better than to think you might care for me. You keep me at arm's length just like my parents did. Only your excuse is your morality and your religion. When you're ready to accept me as I am and," he added in meaning-fraught tones, "*love me*—physically—and not in just some high and mighty spiritual terms, let me know. I might be around."

He picked his coat from the floor and swung it across his shoulder before adding, "And then again, I might not. I've been turning down some enticing opportunities with other women, Pam. Maybe I'll just start taking some of them up on their offers. You see, there's no strings attached and very few demands on a one night stand.

The door closed behind him with the finality of a closing tomb. She shrank back in her seat in horror. *What have I done?*

He was gone. Driven away by her fear, her demands, her rules. She had lost him just as surely as she had lost Michael in that blazing racetrack fire. All she had been doing was protecting herself. Was it already too late to protect herself from Tiger Evans— had he already ensnared her heart so securely?

"Going to the game tonight, Pam?" Rick stopped at her desk and tapped a pencil on its corner.

"I hadn't planned on it."

"What? And not see the famous Tiger Evans play? Are you sick?"

Pam dropped her eyes to her desk so that Rick couldn't see the tears that had sprung there. She *was* sick—sick at heart—over the faltering relationship between she and Ty.

"Well, are you?"

"No, Rick. I just haven't enjoyed the games much lately. They seem, well, different."

"You mean Tiger seems different. I'll agree with that. He's been skating with a vengeance lately. He's picked up more penalties in the past two weeks than in the last two seasons. I saw him take four steps to body check a player last night. He landed in the penalty box for charging, of course. And within minutes he was back in there for high-sticking. He had his stick way above shoulder level and moved into direct confrontation with another skater. That's not like him. Even though he likes a fight, he's always been one of the cleanest players on the ice. I wonder what's bugging him. Does he say anything to you?"

Pam shook her head. As long as Rick didn't realize that she and Ty were estranged, she wouldn't tell him. He would ask too many curious, probing questions. And she didn't want any juicy bits of gossip on Ty's personal life to turn up in the sports pages.

"I'd have thought he'd be in high spirits since he signed that big-bucks advertising and promotional contract last weekend. I heard it came up, and he grabbed it. Has he said anything to you?"

Again Pam shook her head. All she knew of the promotional deal she had read in the paper. Ty had been offered a contract to promote several products including hockey equipment and some type of soda pop for a healthy sum. His name and face would be household commodities by the end of the summer and he would be an even wealthier man.

"Well, do you want to go to the game with me?" The tapping of Rick's pencil finally broke through her reverie.

"Oh, I suppose. I'd like to see how the first promotional gimmicks go. I can't imagine Ty liking all the fuss."

"Maybe not, but there are certain . . . 'things' . . . that make up for it."

"And what does that mean?"

"Have you seen the billboard out on west Portage? Tiger Evans is tying his skates and two beautiful, scantily clad girls in hockey skates are watching him. There's some insipid line about attracting attention when you buy the best equipment, and it finishes, 'Tiger does.' It's pretty sick, but I'll bet it sells a pile of skates. And posing with those girls can't be half bad."

Pamela felt herself fall one more step into the background of Ty's life. What had happened to the sweet, unassuming man who was comfortable in her simple little apartment? Had she driven him to this too?

"Come on, Pam. You look like you need an outing. The game should be fun. There's going to be a reception for Ty afterward. I've got two press passes. We'll go see what it's like to rub shoulders with the great and near-great."

Her curiosity finally won out, and Pam gathered her coat and purse from the locker room and followed Rick to his car. If Ty had changed all that much in the past few weeks, she would have to come to grips with it sometime. She would have to accept that he really *was* gone from her own quiet life and absorbed by the commercial, worldly business community.

"That guy can really play hockey." Awed admiration rang in Rick's voice. "Did you see that flip pass he just made? Perfect control. He just picked it up with the toe of his stick and sailed it right over the defensive player between him and the receiver. Great job!"

Pam hunched back in her chair chewing her bottom lip and regretting that she had ever agreed to come. Painful as it was to see Ty on the ice, she dreaded even more seeing him at the reception after the game. At least while he was on the ice there was no opportunity to speak. If they met later, she might have to engage in the idle small talk that she and Ty had always been able to avoid. It would be another reminder of how the relationship had regressed.

The reception was even worse than she had imagined. Huge posters of Ty and the products he was endorsing were splattered about the room. A fountain of champagne burbled in one corner and a lavish table of canapes filled another.

"Looks like we're here before the guest of honor," Rick commented, picking up a cracker covered with shrimp and cheese.

"Let's go, Rick. I don't like it here."

"Don't like the glitz and glamor? Hey! You'd better get used to it if you're going to hang around with Tiger Evans. This is a big step for him. His name and hockey are going to begin meaning one and the same thing. People love a winner."

Just when Pam had decided to leave and find a taxi

163

home, a noisy crowd burst through the double doors at the far end of the room. Flash bulbs popped and people began to clap. At the center of the flurry was Ty. His curls were still damp from the shower, and he was blinking rapidly in the rash of flashbulbs snapping. He wore a camel-hair jacket that molded to his broad shoulders and a pale cream shirt that accented the golden hues of his skin. His tie was slightly askew, and he was trying to straighten it as he walked.

Each time he got the tie in place, someone would tug on his clothes and muss his efforts. Again and again he smiled patiently and straightened the knot anew.

"They can't keep their hands off him, can they?" Rick whispered into Pam's ear. "Suppose you know the feeling."

Privately enraged at the women surrounding Ty, Pam still couldn't help but watch the blatant forwardness with which they wooed him. Never was there a moment when someone's hand was not resting on his arm or thigh, caressing him over some intimate comment or idle chatter. Pam found her fingers clenching and unclenching as she fought the urge to go and throttle them all—Ty included.

"Why don't we go and say hello? I imagine Tiger will be glad to see you're here." Rick forcibly navigated her toward Ty and the cluster of photographers and women.

Suddenly she felt very overdressed in snug jeans and a woolly fisherman-knit sweater. Most of the dresses here were little more than a drape of sheer fabric and a zipper. But, then again, she hadn't planned to be here at all, or she might have made the effort as well. After all, Ty was worth it.

Coolly, she greeted him. His eyes lit for a moment as they traveled up and down her form, eyeing her casual dress. He smiled and asked, "Going sledding?"

She looked down slightly, having difficulty suppressing the grin that was threatening. "You know me, I always like to be warm. I'll resort to sleeveless dresses in July." Her heart threatened to pummel itself through the wall of her chest. For a moment there seemed to be no one in the room but her and Ty.

Then the crowd began to press in upon them. Pam caught a glimpse of Rick from the corner of his eye, studying them curiously. As she moved to say more to the waiting Ty, a slender, heavily-made up girl insinuated herself between them.

Entwining her fingers in the buttons of Ty's shirt she mewled, "Tiger, darling, I've been trying to get over here for fifteen minutes. It's sweet of you to talk to your little fans," and she shot Pam a scornful glance, "but now I think you should take a little time for me."

Much to Pam's horror, the girl had managed to undo two of Ty's buttons and slide her hand under his shirt where it rested possessively, kneading the soft skin of his chest.

Tactfully Ty took the girl by the wrist and attempted to tug her away, but she would not be deterred. "Don't be shy now, Tiger. You know you love it."

Before Ty had a chance to respond, Pamela swung around and darted for the door. Rick could stay until spring if he wanted. She had to get out with what tiny shreds of dignity she had left.

"Hey! Wait for me!" Rick caught up with her in the hallway. "What just went on in there, anyway?" He was still chewing on a smoked oyster sandwiched between two slices of sausage and held a paper cup of champagne in his other hand.

"I'll get a cab. You can stay and eat to your heart's content. See you at work." She sped off full speed, grateful for the treads on the bottoms of her boots. What she needed now was to be alone. Rick's prying interrogation was most unwelcome. Just as she turned the corner to disappear from sight, his voice came carrying after her down the long, empty corridor.

"Remember what I said about getting a 'scoop' on Tiger Evans, Pam! I think you've got your finger on one and you aren't telling anyone. Remember!"

She cupped her palms over her ears and raced for the door.

At home, Pam sat staring at the panoramic view of the city her apartment afforded. Gnawing disappointment and sadness grew within her. How could she have been so wrong? She choked on a wry, ironic laugh. What an optimistic little fool she had been! She had even gone so far as to compare Ty Evans with Simon Peter—volatile, loving, warmhearted, gifted, impulsive, and imperfect—but a potential tool for God's handiwork.

Imperfect. But no more imperfect than herself. Pam reached for the lesson book she had been using in Pastor Williamson's classes on Peter and scanned the pages.

Thoughtfully, she laid the book on the table. She had forgotten the most important part—God's hand in a man's life. It was He who could win Ty and mold him and ultimately use him as an instrument of His own purpose. Silently she prayed for that moving force in Ty's life. He needed it now more than ever with the complicating seducements she had witnessed.

Finally her anger and resentment left her, as she turned it all over to her Heavenly Father. Whatever was to become of her and Ty was in His hands now. With a peace she hadn't felt since her stormy parting with Ty, she slept.

CHAPTER 10

"GOING TO THE PRESS CONFERENCE, PAM?" Rick singled her out as she darted for the doorway.

"Have to. I'm doing a feature on Rod Steinway, the Blazers' assistant coach. Rumor has it he's been offered a head-coaching position in the States. Maybe it will come up at the conference."

"I doubt it. Everybody focuses on Tiger Evans these days. He's becoming quite a celebrity. Funny, I never expected it of him. Something has happened to change him. He laid low for years. Maybe he's finally realizing that he'd better take advantage of a good thing while he has it."

"What do you mean by that?" As much as she didn't like Rick's chatter, she had to admit that he was on track much of the time.

"He's going to be twenty-nine soon. He won't be playing hockey too many more years. He'd better earn the bucks now, before he retires or gets sidelined with an injury. He's led a charmed life as far as injuries are concerned. Maybe he figures his turn is coming."

"I hardly think that money is one of Ty's concerns," Pam scoffed, remembering his parents' estate. Then she paused for more reflection, "Unless . . ."

"Unless what?"

"Never mind. Come on. You can ride with me." Pam led Rick to the car still pondering the idea that had just occurred to her. Perhaps Ty wasn't going to be in line for whatever wealth his parents had. Their relationship was far from harmonious. She would never forget the look on his father's face that evening in the study—confusion, disgust, hatred. But was that hatred for Ty or for himself?

She was unwilling to think too deeply of Ty today. Seeing him at the press conference would be difficult enough. Her apartment seemed so empty without him. She dearly wished to see one of his big fur coats strewn across her furniture again.

"Hurry up. It's about to start." Rick prodded Pam from the car. They raced through the double doors of the conference room just as several members of the Blazers team entered at the front. Ty was in the midst of them, looking as wonderful as ever. He blinked his golden eyes sleepily at the running camera as if to indicate boredom with the whole affair. But Pam saw them widen slightly before they fell back into sleepy slits as they settled on her and Rick.

She smiled to herself. At least she still had that much of an effect on him. She had difficulty keeping her mind on the questions and answers that ensued and hoped Rick's notes would be adequate for the two of them. Only Ty's comments seemed to make the room come to life for her, and every word he spoke seemed indelibly etched on her memory.

Pam edged her way forward to make contact with Steinway just as Ty turned to leave. Their shoulders brushed in passing. For an electric moment Pam felt as though she had put her finger in a light socket.

Then Ty leaned toward her and whispered, "I've missed you, Prudish Pamela."

He turned away before she could respond, but for the first time in many weeks, Pam saw a glimmer of hope for their deteriorating relationship.

"Are you sure you want to go to the game with me?" Wendy queried. "I know you can sit in the press box if you go alone."

"Don't be silly. I'd love to go with you. I've hardly seen you since Wendell started taking up your time." Pam watched her friend blush with pleasure. She felt a warm glow of her own, feeling partly responsible for throwing them together at her dinner party.

Her dinner party. That seemed eons ago, when she and Ty were enjoying each other's company instead of dancing cautiously around each other like defensive warriors. Only Ty's words of the afternoon kept her from falling into a melancholy mood.

They were late, and the players were already on the ice by the time they arrived.

"You'll have to tell me what's going on," Wendy whispered. "I've never been able to keep up. It all seems to move so fast."

Pam nodded. "Right now they're in an offensive play called headmanning. All they're really trying to do is get the puck to the lead skater in the attack."

"Oh." Wendy nodded sagely. A minute later she leaned over to ask, "Pam, why is that fellow bumping the guy with the puck?"

"He's body checking. When the puck carrier has his head down it's a good time to hit him with a body check. Ty told me that a good body checker looks directly at his victim's chest. Then he maneuvers himself so his own body is in direct line with that chest. The checker pushes off his rear foot and rams the puck carrier with his shoulder and digs it into the other player's chest."

169

"That sounds terrible to me!"

"I know. I've been trying all winter, and I still find it difficult to get used to. It seems so . . . dangerous." The shadowy fear that haunted Pam threatened to surface. She willed her eyes back to the ice and to Ty.

He wasn't involved in the current play, but skating at the fringes, his eyes on the net. Suddenly an opposing skater came behind him, obviously taking Ty by surprise and hit him with a sudden, forceful blow. The referee's whistle blew almost before Ty flew into the boards and crumpled on the ice.

"What happened, Pam? What happened?" Wendy's voice came to her through the screaming of the crowd.

Her eyes never leaving the ice, Pam answered, "They've called an interference, Wendy. That player impeded Ty's progress while he wasn't involved in the active play."

"But Ty isn't getting up!"

A sickening knot was growing in Pam's stomach. She was remembering, word for word, what Ty had said about interferences.

"It's a minor penalty—only two minutes—but, boy, how I hate interferences. You can get a wicked injury that way because you don't expect to be hit. A player can be minding his own business out on the ice away from the action and wham! If you aren't prepared for a hit it's mighty easy to lose your balance."

"There, now he's moving, Pam." Wendy gave a detailed blow-by-blow of the action before them. "But he's grabbing at his leg! He must be hurt!"

Pam's nails dug into her friend's arm as she silently watched the activity on the ice. Most of the arena was on its feet and waiting with baited breath.

Shortly a stretcher was rolled across the ice and Ty lifted onto it. The crowd gave a deafening roar of support as the cart disappeared. As he was carried through the gate, Ty lifted one hand in a weak salute and was rewarded with a riotous round of applause.

"I've got to find out what happened." Pam stood up and grabbed her coat. "Stay here. I'll come back as soon as I can."

She raced down the concrete stairs and through the now-familiar back ways of the arena to an area near the dressing rooms. She could hear men yelling as she neared the door.

"Move back! Give him some air! He's in a lot of pain."

"Hang on, Tiger. We'll have you at the hospital in a few minutes. The ambulance is coming around to the back door."

Pam's heart sank. Her only access to the back door was through the locker room. She raced through the door just as Ty's golden head disappeared through the closing doors of the ambulance, it's fiery globe bathing the night with red.

"Hey! You can't be in here! Oh, . . . it's you, Miss Warren."

Pam came face to face with Rod Steinway. "Rod, how is he? What's wrong?"

"It's his leg. That's all I know, Miss Warren. He was in a lot of pain." Rod's head drooped. "Tiger! Boy, I thought he had a lucky charm that kept him away from all of this."

"Rod, this is off the record, I need to know—is it bad?" Pam waited for the assurances to roll from Steinway's tongue. They never came.

"Could be. Could very well be. You'd better go now, Miss Warren, before someone else comes and kicks you out."

More alarmed than ever, Pam made her way back to Wendy.

"Well, is he going to be all right?" Wendy demanded.

"I don't know. I guess I'll have to call the hospital in the morning."

171

"Can't you go there tonight?"

"I'd only be in the way. I could have a few weeks ago, and I know Tiger would have wanted me, but now I'm not so sure. He's in good hands, Wendy. Anyway, they'll probably give him something to make him sleep. I'll just wait until morning."

But morning took forever to arrive.

After hours of restless churnings, Pam finally dozed off only minutes before her telephone jarred her awake.

"Pam? Rick. Are you awake?"

"I am now. What is it?"

"Did you hear about Evans?"

She bolted upright in her bed. "What? What about him?"

"I talked to a buddy of mine who's in with the coaches. They're afraid that Tiger may never skate again. I guess his knee is really torn up. They've had to sedate him just to keep him calm. Brother, what a loss. Well, gotta go. Just thought you'd like to know. 'Bye."

Pam found herself staring at the phone receiver listening to the strident hum of the line.

He may never skate again. The thought echoed through her head until she began to believe it would drive her mad. Finally she got up and pawed through her closet for something to wear. She had to go to him. Whether he wanted her or not. He needed support. He needed prayer. And she could offer him both.

"Could you tell me what room Ty Evans is in please?" Pam shuffled her feet nervously at the information desk.

"Room 812, but, oh, I'm sorry! Mr. Evans has requested no visitors."

Pam's heart sank. Now what?

172

"If you'd like to talk to the head nurse on his floor perhaps she could give you some information about his condition," the receptionist offered, seeing Pam's sagging shoulders and defeated expression.

"Thank you. I will." Pam shot toward the elevator. Perhaps she would have better luck upstairs.

"I'm sorry, but Mr. Evans has specifically requested no visitors." The nurse checked and rechecked the chart as Pam pleaded with her.

"Well, thank you, anyway. Would you tell him that Pam Warren was here to see him, please?"

"Certainly, Miss Warren. Now if you'll excuse me, I have to begin rounds with the doctors."

"Nurse, is there another exit, or do I have to go back the way I came?" Pam felt as if she had been traveling in a maze to get this far and dreaded the trip back.

The white-frocked woman smiled. "It is a rather confusing trek to the surgical ward. But there's another elevator at the end of this hall. It will take you down to the back door of the hospital."

"Thanks!" Pam turned toward the nurse's pointing finger and walked slowly down the hall. Tears began to drip down her cheeks as she dragged her feet toward the exit. It was horrible to think of Ty here, changed from robust and healthy to . . . what?

Pam glanced up as she neared the exit sign. Directly across from the metal door was a room. Room 812. The door stood ajar and through it Pam could see the foot of the bed.

Furtively she glanced back toward the nurses' station, but it was vacant. On impulse she stepped toward the room. If she could just have a glimpse of Ty she would feel so much better—just a glimpse.

The room was small and seemed smaller still filled with pulleys and supports and all forms of unfamiliar equipment. Ty lay in the narrow bed, his knee supported somehow from beneath, a tent-like affair covering it. His head was turned away from the door, his right arm flung across his cheek and forehead.

Regretting her presence, Pam backed away again to escape into the hall, but her toe caught on the tip of a three-legged IV stand and she stumbled.

"Now what?" Ty rolled toward the sound. "I'm getting sick of being poked and prod . . . Pam? Go away." He flung his arm back across his face and turned his head toward the wall.

Pam's heart wrenched in pity. He couldn't even turn his back to her because of whatever supported his knee. For once Tiger Evans was completely defenseless.

"I'm sorry, Ty. I know you didn't want visitors. I just wanted to look at you and then leave. I caught my toe on something or you wouldn't have heard me.

"You wanted to look at me?" Ty rolled toward her again, his face contorted with pain and rage. "Well, *look* then! Look good and hard! Do you like it? I hope you watched me skate last night, Pam, because," and his voice broke, and he turned back to the wall, "it's the last time anyone is ever going to see me skate again."

He buried his face in his pillow, and Pam could see his shoulders quivering with contained emotion. Instinctively she stepped closer, but was stopped short by his muffled words, "Go away, Pam. Just go away."

Retreating, Pam whispered, "But if you need me, I'll come, Ty. Remember that. And I'll be praying."

His silence answered her, and she hurried to the exit to make her escape. Escape. That was something else Ty Evans couldn't do anymore.

"Hello, Miss Warren. I suppose you're here for our interview." Rod Steinway leaned back in his desk and put his feet across the piles of papers and envelopes.

"More or less, I guess. I'm afraid my heart isn't in

it. How about yours?" Pam shrugged the backpack off her shoulder and sunk into the battered wooden chair beside his desk.

"No, not really. Do you have any news about Tiger? I suppose until we get a final word on him this whole team will be in the dumps. It's like everything else, I guess. You don't appreciate what you have until you lose it."

"You mean Ty?"

"And what he gave this team, Pam. He was everyone's hero and everyone's champion. If any man on this team was having a bad night, Tiger would give him such a pep talk the fellow wouldn't dare do anything but play his best! He rallied this team on more than one occasion when things looked bad. Granted, he isn't perfect, but the type of enthusiasm he displayed was something else again."

"And now he's lost it."

"All of it. I finally finagled my way in to see him last night. I think I was the first one he'd even talked to since he'd had surgery on the knee. He's refused to see anyone—his friends, his teammates, his parents. He's bitter, Pam. He's not the same man."

Pam sighed. Rod's words only confirmed what she already feared. Ty had rejected everyone and everything. Especially God. And it was Him that Ty needed most right now.

"So what happens next?"

"Well, the doctors won't be sure of the results of his surgery for a while yet. He'll have to get back into shape too. Lying around in a hospital bed isn't great for muscle tone. Ty said he was getting out soon. He can't do steps yet. But what surprised me most of all is that he said he was moving home for a few weeks."

"Home?" Pam shot upright in her chair. "He's going *home*?"

"Yeh. That amazed me too. From what little he's said, I thought he and his parents didn't get along. I suppose he needs someone to help him out."

And it should be me. Pam left Steinway's office after the interview and wandered aimlessly about the empty arena. Ty was taking giant steps backward. Pam longed for the happy days of their relationship and the long, loving conversations they had had. She had talked of her faith, and Ty had seemed guardedly receptive. Especially after she had given him the Bible.

She had been sure then that the seeds she had planted had fallen on fertile ground. Now, she was beginning to discover, perhaps that ground had been shallow and rocky instead. Whatever progress Ty had made in life he seemed bent on destroying. Moving into his father's house could only speed that process.

It was as though Tiger Evans had disappeared from the face of the earth. No one could get through to him at his own apartment or his parents'. A maid with a memorized speech deterred all callers.

Finally it occurred to Pam that there *might* be a place that she could accost Ty and speak to him. Packing her swimsuit and a leotard in a small duffle bag, she set out for the gym where Ty had taken her swimming. Her hunch was rewarded when she saw the red Porsche parked discreetly at the back of the building.

Hurrying into a hot pink leotard, Pam clasped a turquoise belt at her waist and headed for the weight room. He was there. Thinner, leaner, more subdued. Sweat was pouring from his body in rivulets as he worked the injured knee. He gritted his teeth, eyes closed, every muscle tensed. Pam could feel the effort he put into every lift of the leg and sense every shudder of relief as he lowered it.

She had not even begun to realize the physical anguish Ty must have experienced. And it was obviously not over yet. He gripped the sides of the bench until his knuckles whitened and his body shook and pressed onward.

Helpless to alleviate his physical pain, Pam closed her eyes and prayed—for Ty, for herself, for the words he needed to hear. Her petition complete, she opened them to find Ty watching her with an aching bleakness that tore at her heart. The golden eyes were umber with pain and despair. A palpable barrier seemed erected between them.

Frightened by the despondence and resentment in his eyes, Pamela turned and ran. Tears streamed down her cheeks as she cowered in the locker room. For the first time, she was afraid of the Tiger.

The season was winding down. The Blazers stood well in the rankings. Not so near the top as they had hoped, but not so low as they had feared after losing Ty Evans. It was nearly April, and the winter was wearing out. Only in bitter outbursts did it sputter its power. Most days were sunny and clear and finally Pam ventured outside without trepidation.

One wet and drippy day, Pam felt the restless pull of spring fever. Slipping into her car, she began to drive. She meandered through narrow streets with houses built nearly wall to wall. Then she ventured toward the river. Soon she found herself on the street that held the Evan's mansion. Feeling purposeful in her aimlessness, Pam found herself at the familiar gate, staring at the prepossessing home.

She parked the car and stared at the silent structure, searching for a glimpse of life. It had been over six weeks since she had seen Ty in the gym.

"Are you lost?" The voice came from behind her. Pam jumped so that her head nudged the window frame with a soft crack.

"No, I'm just—Ty!"

Leaning on a burled wood cane and smiling slightly, Ty Evans was the most welcome sight of all.

"Are you okay?"

"Fine." Pam rubbed the top of her head. "It's a

177

good thing I bumped myself there—it's my hardest spot."

"Mine too. But you should know that. Want to take a walk with me? I'm slow, but steady."

Pam swung her legs eagerly from the car. "I'd love to. I have spring fever. I seem to move from one malady to another—cabin fever all winter, now spring fever. What comes with summer?"

Ty chuckled low in his throat. Pam had nearly forgotten that musical sound. It made her heady with glee.

"Am I going too fast?" She eyed his progress.

"No. I go at this pace until I get to the end of the block and out of my mother's sight. Then I speed up. Otherwise she sends the maid out after me to slow me down. It's pretty funny, actually. The maid has lost five pounds chasing me down the street."

Pam giggled. "You look terrific."

"So do you. I'd nearly forgotten what a great body was under all those layers."

"I must confess I laundered the long johns for the last time this season. They're at the bottom of my drawer with my wool cardigans."

"Have you put your coat into storage yet?"

"No. I wasn't sure where to take it." Pam was astounded by the easy, relaxed conversation. She dared not become too serious for fear of shattering the moment.

"Take it to one of Dad's stores. Don't keep it out over the summer."

"If you say so."

"I do."

They stopped mid-sidewalk and stared at each other, hungry for each other's faces. Pam stood breathlessly as Ty leaned toward her and planted a tender kiss on her open lips.

"Um. I'd forgotten how good that tastes." He licked his lips appreciatively and began to walk again.

"Ty—"

"I know, I know. What's come over me? Right? What happened to the angry, bitter, hockey player?"

"I don't miss him, but I'd like to know where he went," Pam admitted.

"He's still here. But he's under control again. I'm sorry for the way I treated you, Pam. It was a terrible time for me but I treated you like dirt."

"It's okay, Ty. Forget it."

"I can't. I discovered some facets of myself that I didn't like. There was a little more of my father in me than I cared to admit. More anger. More insecurity."

"What about your father, Ty? How can you live here with him? I was stunned when Rod told me you'd moved back home."

"I'm sure you were. I was desperate, actually. I hated it in the hospital, but I couldn't be alone. And mother promised me that things had changed."

"Changed? How?" Their steps slowed even further as they talked.

"I have you partly to thank for that, I guess. It all started the night that you were at the house for dinner. My mother knew my father punished me unmercifully as a child, but she never dreamed the extent of the abuse. She's weak, Pam. She suspected but she never dared ask questions. But the night you caught my father going after me with the poker triggered something in him. He'd been found out. And if nothing else is important to my father, public opinion is. He went into counseling." Ty nodded at Pam's dumbstruck face. "I know. I didn't believe it either. But he has. And it seems to be helping. I've been in the house several weeks, and we haven't come to blows once. We've even had a conversation or two."

"That's wonderful!"

"Let's just say that I'm guardedly optimistic. I've got too many scars to forget about them all. But I suppose I can forgive him."

179

She looked at him curiously. He had changed. The wild, restlessness that haunted him seemed gone. It was a placid Tiger that remained.

"Something else has been going on with you, Ty Evans. I don't feel like I even recognize you any more!"

Ty smiled. "I had a lot of time to think in the past weeks, Pam. And I had a lot to get used to."

"Not skating?"

He nodded. "I was sure my career was over, but I didn't want to let go. I finally had to, Pam. And when I did, well, that's the ironic part."

"What do you mean?"

"I'd finally resolved myself to never skating again. I'd even managed to watch a Blazer game on television and talk to some of the guys about it. Then this big team of doctors calls me in and tell me that they think I *can* skate next year. And the next, if I want to."

"If you *want* to?"

"Yes. And you had a part in this, too, Pam."

"I didn't realize I had so much influence from a distance."

"Well, you do. It was because of you that I finally came to accept the fact that hockey didn't have to be my whole life. You showed me that there's more to life than skating. When I look back on it, I must have scared you a little, Prudish Pamela. I seem to remember being a bit wild and rowdy for you."

"Let's just say you were a change of pace from the boys I knew at church back home."

Ty tipped his head back and laughed. "You were a change of pace for me, too. I'd never known a girl to whom it would even *occur* to give me a Bible! Sometimes I wondered if I'd picked up a throwback to ancient days!"

"Gee, thanks." Pam scuffed her toe along the sidewalk.

"No, . . . thank *you*. I began to wonder if maybe I couldn't be more of a service to young people as a Christian athlete than as the rough and tumble standard I'd been in the past. Your quiet faith impressed me, Pam. But I didn't know what to do about it."

"Ty—"

"No, let me finish. I know this all sounds crazy and mixed-up to you, but I have to explain. I met a fellow in therapy, a football player, who'd gotten busted up in a car accident. He was even less likely than I was to get back into his profession. But he wasn't angry. He said that if he couldn't play football, he'd do something else. It didn't matter what, he said, just so it was done for the right reasons. I drilled him about it. He said something that struck me so profoundly that I haven't forgotten it. He said, 'Whatever you do, work at it with all your heart, as working for the Lord, not for men.' That's called having your priorities straight, Pam. I didn't. Not then. But I'm working on it."

Pam struggled to speak but the words wouldn't come. Her heart's desire had been answered and her tongue had lost its will. But the words of Pastor Williamson on the last day of their study of Simon Peter sang in her head. "The life of Simon Peter proves to us that God can work with frail humanity and pull it far beyond itself to greater love and service." It had happened to Ty. He, like Peter, had been won by love, schooled by hardship and adversity, and would ultimately be used by God as an instrument of His purpose.

"Are you crying?" Ty leaned into Pam's face and waved a pristine white handkerchief near her nose.

"No—yes—I don't know!"

"Well, use the handkerchief. You've got the waterworks going, whatever the cause."

Still snuffling into the lime-scented cloth, Pam murmured, "But what about skating?"

181

"I don't know. Rod Steinway was by a few days ago. He is going to take that head coaching job we've been hearing rumors about. He offered me his assistant coach's position. They had a meeting and agreed unanimously to hire me if I want to take it. He feels that the head coach will be retiring at the end of next season, and I can step into his shoes if I want to. I'll have to think about it. Maybe even pray," and he winked at the red-eyed girl, "like someone else I know always does."

Speechless, Pam threw her arms about his neck and nearly toppled both of them onto the concrete.

"Whoa! I don't have the balance I used to, Pamela! You'll take us both out of the game with a move like that! How about," and he ran an exploratory finger along her cheek, "driving us over to my apartment? I have a sudden desire to be out from under the prying eyes of my mother's maid! Unless, of course, you're afraid to enter a place as perilous as a Tiger's lair?"

"Somehow, I think this is one Tiger who's been tamed," she retorted gleefully. Then, serious again, she continued, "But, Ty, would you be very disappointed to give up skating for coaching—now that you have the choice?" She watched his golden eyes, looking for a sign of his true feeling.

But they lit with laughter, and she felt his free arm around her waist and the tip of the cane nudging her toe. "I'm getting too old to be a hockey player, Pam. I think I should get into something I'm the right age for—like being a husband and a father. I think it's time for this old Tiger to settle down and raise some cubs. Think you could help me with a project like that?"

Pam heard the clatter of his cane as it fell to the concrete and felt his other arm come around her in a loving embrace. Finally there were no more shadows to haunt them. And soon she would be living in the most dangerous and wonderful spot on earth—a Tiger's lair.

About the Author

Judy Baer was born and raised in North Dakota. She started writing when her youngest daughter was three and old enough to sit on her lap and punch the space bar on the typewriter between words. Now, ten years later and with over 35 novels to her credit, Judy is typing her own spaces between words—for books that include inspirational romances, young adult and middle grade fiction, her own Young Adult series and her first non-fiction book written for teens.

She has received many awards for her writing including several first place in fiction awards from the National Federation of Press Women and the Silver Diary award from the Young Adult Network for contributions to young adult literature.

A Letter To Our Readers

Forever Romances are inspirational romances designed to bring you a joyful, heart-lifting reading
experience. If you would like more information about
joining our Forever Romance book series, please write
to us:

> Guideposts Customer Service
> 39 Seminary Hill Road
> Carmel, NY 10512

Forever Romances are chosen by the same staff that
prepares *Guideposts,* a monthly magazine filled with
true stories of people's adventures in faith. *Guideposts*
is not sold on the newsstand. It's available by subscrip-
tion only. And subscribing is easy. Write to the
address above and you can begin reading *Guideposts*
soon. When you subscribe, each month you can count
on receiving exciting new evidence of God's Presence,
His Guidance and His limitless love for all of us.